THE STORM

SAMANTHA TOWLE

OTHER CONTEMPORARY NOVELS BY SAMANTHA TOWLE

When I Was Yours

Trouble

REVVED SERIES
Revved
Revived

THE STORM SERIES
The Mighty Storm
Wethering the Storm
Taming the Storm

PARANORMAL ROMANCES BY SAMANTHA TOWLE

The Bringer

THE ALEXANDRA JONES SERIES
First Bitten
Original Sin

Jake and Tru, I know you're fictional...but to me, you are real.
And you changed my life in ways I never imagined possible.
Thank you.

CONTENTS

O
N
E

Fuck, I'm hot. Why am I so hot? My arm is dead, and—what is that in my mouth? Hair?

It's definitely hair.

Belle.

She's in our bed again.

I push the mass of curly black hair from my face and mouth. I stare down at my sleeping three-year-old daughter and chuckle.

She must've got in our bed during the night.

I glance over at the empty space beside me.

Tru must already be downstairs with the boys.

I can barely remember the time when my life wasn't like this, when my life was empty and lonely.

Now, it's filled with everything I never imagined I could have.

Tru, and she has given me a life beyond my dreams, and three beautiful, amazing children—JJ, Billy, and Belle.

This, right here, is fucking perfection. My life is perfection.

I know how lucky I am. I know because there was a time when my life wasn't perfect.

But that was then, and this is now. And now is awesome.

Guess I'd better haul my ass out of bed. I've got a meeting at the label this morning. I'll leave my little sleeping Beauty, so she can get a few more minutes of shut-eye before I wake her.

I slip my arm out from underneath Belle as carefully as I can. Then, I quietly climb out of bed and make my way to the bathroom.

I'm just mid piss when I hear my baby girl's sleepy voice from behind me, "Dada, why I not have a peenis?"

Shifting to the side so that I'm covering myself from Belle's view, I glance over my shoulder, a chuckle escaping me. "'Cause you're a girl, Beauty."

"But I wanna be a boy, like you, JJ, and Billy." She juts her lips out, pouting. "I wanna peenis!"

She's standing there, demanding a penis, in her Disney princess pajamas, with her arms folded across her chest, her foot tapping.

God, she is exactly like her mother. Not that Tru ever wanted a cock—well, aside from mine inside her, of course.

But Belle has Tru's steely determination, and she looks exactly like her mother, which means trouble for me when she's older.

But like I know how to handle my wife's temperament, I know how to handle Belle.

"Okay, Beauty, how about this?" I say in a pacifying tone, holding in my laughter. I tuck myself back into my pajama pants and go to wash my hands. "Why don't you ask Santa for a penis for Christmas?" The second that I've said it, I know that it sounds all kinds of wrong. It's so wrong that I wish to God I could take it back.

"Santa, give me a peenis!" Belle starts squealing, jumping around and clapping her hands.

"Fuck. Shit! No!" I panic as soon as the words leave my mouth, knowing exactly what Belle is like.

A goddamn parrot is what she's like.

"Fuck! Shit! Santa, peenis!" Belle starts to mimic, hands still clapping together.

Crap. Tru is going to kill me. Kill me dead.

"Christ." I cover my face with my hands. "Belle, no."

I reach down and pick her up. She wraps her little chubby legs around my hips, her hands clutching at my neck.

"Don't say those words. Bad words." I touch my fingertip to her nose, staring into her big brown eyes—Tru's eyes.

"Fuck. Sh—"

"Bad words," I reiterate, giving her a serious look. "We do not repeat those words. Ever. And especially not in front of Mommy. Okay?"

"So, Santa gimme peenis if I say no bad wowds?"

"Oh God," I groan.

"Santa! Peenis!" She giggles.

"Breakfast, Belle!" I exclaim. "You want some Frozen cereal?" I say to distract her.

That fucking annoying Disney film is her favorite, and she will only eat that particular brand of cereal.

"Fwozen!" she shrieks.

Then, she launches into the chorus of "Let It Go" as I carry her out of the bathroom, heading downstairs to the kitchen where my tribe should be.

By the time I reach the bottom step, I've actually joined in singing along with her. When you've heard that fucking song played a trillion times, it's hard not to sing it.

"Mama!" Belle yells the instant we enter the kitchen. "Dada say Santa gimme peenis on Chwissmas!"

Fuck.

Tru's eyes meet mine. "Did he now?"

I see a tickle of a small smile at the corner of her mouth.

I grin, shrugging. "What my baby girl wants, my baby girl gets."

I set Belle in her seat at the breakfast bar.

"Morning, JJ, Billy." I kiss the tops of my boys' heads, their eyes glued on the TV.

I get a, "Morning," from Billy and a grunt from JJ.

I head over to Tru, who is buttering toast, and I slip my arms around her waist. Turning her to face me, I cup her ass, which is now out of the kids' view, and I give it a firm squeeze. "Morning," I whisper as I press my lips to hers.

God, she feels good. She always feels good.

"Morning." She kisses me back, her hand pressing against my bare chest. "And good luck explaining to Belle why she didn't get a penis from Santa on Christmas Day."

She laughs softly as I glide my lips over hers again, the sound vibrating down to my cock.

"She'll have forgotten by then." I stare deep into Tru's eyes.

"Yeah, sure, she will. Just like she forgot about when you told her you'd buy her a pink Ferrari for her third birthday."

Shit. I forgot about that.

Belle pitched a total fit when she realized there was no pink Ferrari.

I might spoil Belle a bit. Well, I might spoil all my kids. But when you had nothing as a kid, you want to give yours everything.

"So, Mum and Dad said they'll have the kids tonight, and I thought we could go out…or stay in." Tru runs her finger down my chest to my stomach, stopping just above the waistband of my pajama bottoms.

Of course, my cock sits up and pays attention. He always pays attention to Tru.

"If I get a vote in this, I vote on staying in, and no clothes are allowed for the whole night."

She smiles, a light flickering in her eyes. "Stay in and no clothes, it is."

"Mama! Bweakfast!" Belle squeals.

Chuckling, Tru shakes her head.

"She wants cereal," I tell Tru. "I'll get it." I give her one last lingering kiss.

"Bweakfast!" Belle yells again.

Releasing a sigh, I let go of Tru but not before giving her fine ass another squeeze. I grab the cereal from the cupboard and then get Belle's princess bowl and favorite spoon. I pour the cereal and milk, and then I take the bowl over to her.

Look at me, the model of domesticity.

"What do we say, Belle?"

"Tank you, Dada." She smiles up at me before digging into her cereal.

God, she's cute. No wonder I'm putty in that little girl's hands.

"You want coffee, babe?" I ask Tru.

"Sure."

I pour us both coffee and take hers over to her while she busies herself with making lunch for the boys in between eating her toast.

"You want me to do anything?" I ask her.

"Nah, I'm good."

"You want me to take the boys to school on my way to the label?"

"Mum and Dad are taking them."

Tru's mom and dad, Eva and Billy, are a godsend.

They live in LA now. I got them a house just down the street from us.

With the kids' school and my studio being here, we're here more than we are in the UK. Eva and Billy wanted to be closer to the kids and us, so they moved to LA a few years ago.

"What are you doing today?" I ask Tru.

"I've got a conference call with Vicky in an hour. Then, Belle and I are having a girlie day, pampering in preparation for our night."

She gives me a sexy wink, and I feel it in the base of my cock, my balls tightening up.

Leaning in close, touching my chest to her shoulder, I whisper in her ear, "I can't wait to fuck you tonight."

Tru and I don't get to have sex as much as we used to now that we have three kids, I have a label to run and a band to record and tour with, and Tru has her magazine.

Tru opened up an LA division of *Etiquette*. She and Vicky are business partners. Vicky runs the UK base, and Tru heads the US one.

So, kids and work combined don't leave us much alone time. When we do have alone time, we make the most of it. And I intend on making the absolute most of the time we have tonight. I'll be fucking her until neither of us can walk.

"God, Jake." She shudders and then turns to face me, pressing those fantastic tits of hers up against my chest. "I can't wait either."

My cock starts to stiffen. "I'm gonna fuck you so hard—"

"Mom, can you get me some more juice?" That's Billy.

And down my dick goes.

God, my kids are total cockblockers.

But this is our life— stolen moments with each other and permanent interruptions from the kids. Honestly, I wouldn't trade it for the world.

"Tonight. You and me. Fucking hard. All night long. Don't plan on getting any sleep," I quietly tell her before pressing a firm kiss on her lips. Then, I take my coffee with me and head for the shower.

TWO

I'm on a call with Zane, the vice president of my label, when Stuart walks into my office.

Stuart, my assistant, is basically the guy who keeps my life in order, and he has saved my ass more times than I can count. He's also one of my best friends.

The instant I see Stuart's face, I know that something's wrong. I watch him approach my desk and sit down in the chair opposite me.

I quickly wrap up the call with Zane and place my cell on the desk.

"What's up?" I ask Stuart.

He presses his lips together and exhales a breath through his nose. "I just finished a call with a lawyer."

That's no biggie. We get calls from lawyers all the time.

"So? What is it? A copyright lawsuit or some other ridiculous shit?"

"No. It's…" He stops and fidgets in his seat.

He's stalling. I hate it when he stalls because that means it's something big.

"Just spit it out, for fuck's sake," I tell him.

"It's a paternity suit."

"Paternity suit?" I frown. "Against who?"

"You. A paternity suit has been filed against you, Jake."

"I'm sorry, what?" I shake my head.

Then, the words sink in fast, and the bottom drops out of my perfect world. I get angry, really fucking angry. Fear and rage tear through my veins.

"That's bullshit!" I yell. "This is just some idiot trying to get a payday! It's impossible, for one thing. I *always* wore condoms. I never had sex without one." Tru is the only person I haven't used them with. "So, you can tell this gold digger and her lawyer to fuck the hell off!"

"Condoms aren't infallible, Jake."

I scowl at Stuart, and he releases a sigh. Tipping his head back, he runs his hand through his hair. When he looks at me again, I see it written all over his face—there's more.

"There's something else," he says quietly. "The suit isn't filed just against you. There's one against—fuck, how do I say this?"

"You just fucking say it," I snap again.

I don't mean to snap, but it's kind of hard not to right now. And Stuart knows me. He knows how I am. He knows I don't mean it.

"Jonny," he breathes the name out.

My heart stops.

"The suit is also filed against Jonny. Same woman. She's not sure who the father is—you or Jonny."

Jonny. My dead best friend.

"What the actual fuck? How can she file against Jonny? Jesus Christ!" Standing, I shove my chair back and it slams into the wall behind me.

"Do you remember a girl named Tiffany Slater?" Stuart asks.

Tiffany Slater. I toss the name around my head and come up dry.

"No," I growl.

"I remember her. She was part of that group of girls in the early days. I drove her home a few times. She was sweet. Blonde hair. She stuck in my mind because...well, she suddenly dropped off the radar, stopped coming around."

"Plenty of girls stopped coming around when they realized they weren't getting anything more than a fuck from me."

"She was one of the girl's that you and Jonny used to share."

"I don't remember her!" I yell. "I screwed a lot of women back then! Jonny and I shared a lot of women! You know that! Doesn't mean I knocked any of them up!" I drag my hands through my hair. "So, what? She's claiming that her kid is either mine or...Jonny's?"

It's right then, right as I say those words, that the ramifications of what this could mean hit me.

If that kid is mine...

Tru.

I don't want anything to come between us.

But...if that kid is Jonny's, then it means...it means I'll get a piece of him back.

I slowly sink down into my chair.

"Jonny," I breathe out his name, my eyes meeting Stuart's.

"Yeah," he says quietly.

I know he's thinking the same thing.

I rub my eyes with the palms of my hands. "How old is the kid?"

"He's thirteen."

"He?"

"Yeah. His name is Storm."

I let out a humorless laugh. "Original." I lean back in my chair, dragging my hands down my face. "So, why now? Why claim paternity after all these years?"

Discomfort flickers over Stuart's face, and his hands curl around the arms of his chair. "She's…dying, and she is the only family he has."

"Jesus Christ," I exhale. "What's"—*killing her*—"wrong with her?"

"Cancer," Stuart says quietly.

I stare at the wall behind Stuart. A hundred thoughts speed through my mind. The solemnness in the room is silently eating away at me.

"So, now what?" I quietly ask him.

"I call Jonny's dad. I'm sure his lawyer will have spoken to him by now. Then, we arrange for this DNA test that they're asking for. And I make sure this doesn't get leaked to the press."

"And…what do I do?"

Stuart gives me a steady look. "You go home and tell Tru."

Fear curls in the pit of my stomach. Resting my elbows on my desk, I run my hands through my hair. "How do I tell her this?"

"Gently. You tell her gently, Jake."

"This is gonna hurt her—badly."

"It will, but she's strong. You've both gotten through worse."

I know he's referring to Tru's car accident—when she almost died, when I was close to losing her.

I can't lose Tru, no matter what.

12

Tru, JJ, Billy, and Belle—they are everything to me. *Everything.*

My life is perfect. Fucking perfect. I have the woman of my dreams and the best kids a man could ask for. And now this? It's going to rip all of that apart.

When I woke up this morning, surrounded by the most important people in my life, little did I know I'd be hearing this potentially, life-changing news a few hours later.

I guess I can never escape my past. It was destined to come back and haunt me in one way or another.

"I'm gonna go make these calls." Stuart stands. "Anything I can do before I go?"

I move my eyes back to his face and shake my head.

"It's going to be okay, Jake. You'll do this DNA test. We'll find out that he's not yours, and then everything will go back to normal."

"And what if…" I can barely bring myself to say the words because, yeah, there is hope in me. "What if he's Jonny's?"

"Then…" A small smile touches his lips. "Then, our world is about to get a whole lot brighter."

And if Storm is not Jonny's and he is in fact mine, then my world is about to get a whole lot darker.

THREE

Standing in the doorway, I watch her...the first, last and only woman I will ever love.

Tru.

She's barefoot in the kitchen, hips swaying to the sound of Etta James's "At Last," as she softly sings along while uncorking a bottle of wine.

And my heart fucking breaks at the sight.

It breaks because I know I'm about to break hers.

I'm about to put a crack in the life we've built together.

I just pray to God that fissure isn't too deep that we can't keep it together.

She turns, seeing me. "Hey!" She looks a little surprised. "I didn't realize you were home. What are you doing, standing there, watching me?" The smile on her face is warm and wanting and everything.

She is everything.

"So, the kids are at Mum and Dad's. I thought I'd get the wine ready." She starts to walk toward me, her feet padding softly across the floor.

When she reaches me, she places her hands on my chest and pushes up on her toes. "Hi," she whispers on a smile before pressing her lips on mine.

She tastes like heaven.

I have to tell her. But first…

I take her face in my hands, and I kiss her hard. I kiss her with the force of every year that I have loved this woman.

I want her to feel how much I love her…before I hurt her.

"Wow," she whispers, her breathing unsteady. "I guess you really want me, huh?"

God, I want her.

The teasing smile on her lips should be inviting, but all it does is hurt, making this so much harder.

I rub the tips of my fingers across her forehead, brushing back her hair. "We need to talk."

"Can it wait? We have a children-free night, and—"

"It can't wait." My tone is firm. Before I lose my nerve, I take hold of her hand and lead her over to the breakfast stools, the stools where my kids eat breakfast every morning.

God, I feel sick.

I can feel Tru's eyes on me, but I can barely look at her.

She sits up on a stool. "So, what do we need to talk about?" Her voice is unsteady.

I hear the waver, the nerves in her tone.

I'm nervous, too—no, scrap that. *Nervous* doesn't even touch it. I'm fucking terrified.

Swallowing down, I unbutton the top button on my shirt, loosening the collar with my fingers. Then, I meet her eyes.

"We had a call today from a lawyer." Pausing—well, more like delaying—I swallow down.

Tru's eyes, hawk-like, are watching me. It's almost like she's trying to read the words on my face before I say them.

I take a deep breath and force the words out. "It's about a woman...and a kid—a boy. The woman, his mother—she's claiming that...well, that he's...mine...or Jonny's."

I watch as my words hit her. It's like a physical strike. She recoils back as her hand reaches for the counter, gripping it.

Shock morphs into hurt, and pain pulls at her features.

I force myself to hold steady even though all I really want to do is break down and grab her, hold her, tell her how sorry I am.

"How old is the boy?"

That's the first thing she wants to ask me? It's not what I expected her to say.

Then, it hits me why she's asking that.

She wants his age, so she'll know if I've cheated on her during the time we've been together.

Anger wells inside me. But getting pissed off with Tru right now is neither wise nor necessary. It's not like I'm in the position to kick off with the moral high ground.

I have just dropped the bombshell that I'm being sued for paternity.

"He's thirteen," I say through gritted teeth.

I see a small amount of relief briefly flicker through her eyes.

Smoothing her hands down her thighs, she blows out a breath. Then, she shifts to the side and gets up from the stool. On her feet, she walks across the kitchen. She turns off the music. Then, she stands there, her hands pressed on the counter, facing away from me.

"Tru...talk to me."

"What do you want me to say?" She spins around, her face now hard. Anger flares in those eyes I love so much, pain dancing around the edges of them. "Congratulations? Am I supposed to congratulate you on becoming a father again?"

"Don't..." I angrily work my jaw, looking away from her. "I'm not a father again. I'm only a father to our children, the *only* children I have." I bite each word out.

"Not according to this woman!" she yells, throwing her hands up in the air. When they come back down, they slap against her thighs.

"An accusation. That's all it is, Tru. It's not even an accusation. It's just a..."

"A, what, Jake? What is it? All I'm hearing right now is that you could have another child with another woman!"

"He's not mine. I know he isn't." I stare steadily into her eyes. "And it's not just me she's claiming against. It's Jonny, too."

"And that's just fucking great! This woman is claiming that either you or your dead best friend knocked her up all those years ago. I mean, what the hell? You fucked the same women—actually, you know what? I don't want to know!"

She presses her hands to her ears, violently shaking her head for a moment. Then, her hands drop, and her eyes lower to her feet.

"Why now? What does she want?" she whispers.

I can hear the tears in her words, and my chest feels like it's cracking open.

"She's dying." I clear my throat. "And she's the only family the kid has. Maybe she's...I don't know. Maybe she's looking for someone to take care of him when she's gone."

Tru's eyes snap up to mine. They're angry and filled with tears. She swipes at them, her lips curling in disgust— at me presumably. I can feel her contempt like a hand around my throat, choking me.

"I honestly don't know what the hell to do with this, Jake. I mean, I just…I need to get out of here. I need some time to think." She marches through the kitchen, heading for the door.

As she passes me, I grab her arm, stopping her. "Tru, wait. Please. Just stay and talk to me."

"No." She yanks her arm from mine, meeting my stare. Her eyes are laced with venom. "You are the last person I want to talk to right now. I've heard enough from you to last me a fucking lifetime."

I watch her walk out of the kitchen. Then, I hear the front door slam, and her car engine revs a minute later.

And I don't go after her.

I let her go.

FOUR

My cigarette lights the dark around me as I take a drag on it. It's my sixth cigarette since Tru left a few hours ago.

I've had to force myself not to go to where I know she is—at Simone and Denny's.

Simone is Tru's best friend. She's married to one of my best friends and the drummer in my band, Denny.

Of course I know where she is. I always know where Tru is. I have GPS tracking on her cell and car—and not in a creepy way. She knows. It's because of the accident and the fact that Tru and the kids are prime targets for fans and stalkers because of who I am.

Right now, Dave, my trusted bodyguard, is sitting outside of Denny's house, watching and making sure she's okay.

Not that she's okay. I'm not okay.

But I'm hoping she will be, eventually.

Right now, I'm trying to give her the space she asked for. I know she needs time to think this out. It's just how Tru is.

And I know Denny doesn't know about the paternity suit. If he did, he would have called me by now.

I don't want to keep it from him or Tom Carter, the bassist in my band and another one of my best friends. I got lucky when it came to friends.

Both Tom and Denny deserve to know because this involves Jonny, too, but I just want to talk to Tru and then get this fucking DNA test done before I talk to anyone else about it.

I mean, what's the point of talking about the what-ifs? Might as well know the outcome and then talk about that, deal with that.

I just…I know this kid isn't mine.

But…I want him to be Jonny's. This kid, whose mother is dying, I'm wishing that his father, who also suffered that same fate, is Jonny because the selfish part of me wants a piece of my best friend back.

Is that wrong?

I flick the ash from my cigarette into the makeshift ashtray on the floor between my feet. It's actually one of Tru's ceramic bowls that she usually fills with some scented shit. Well, the scented shit is gone, and it's now filled with ash and cigarette butts.

Although I understand her need to walk out, it doesn't mean I'm not frustrated and pissed off.

So, yeah, ruining one of her ceramic bowls has made me feel a little better.

THE STORM

There was a time when, if I'd gotten some fucked-up news or something had happened to piss me off, I would have gotten trashed and broken some stuff, caused some damage to make myself feel better.

Now, I get off on fucking up Tru's shitty little scented bowl.

Pathetic, I know.

I pick up my glass perched beside me on the sun lounger I'm sitting on and take a sip of whiskey.

I don't really drink or smoke much nowadays. I stopped smoking not long after JJ was born. But fuck if I didn't need one tonight. So, I pulled out the emergency pack I had kept stashed away, and had at it.

I put the glass down on the floor beside the ashtray before taking another pull on my cigarette. I blow out the smoke and stare out at the flickering lights of LA, wishing for a lot of things.

Wishing for my past to have been different. Wishing for this not to be happening now. Wishing my past wasn't yet again hurting Tru. Wishing Jonny were still alive.

Music starts to filter through the speakers outside from the internal system we have set up in the house—"Never Tear Us Apart" by INXS. I know Tru is home, and I know she's talking to me. Music—it's how we always talk. And I'm taking this song as a good sign.

I glance over my shoulder, and she's standing in the doorway. She looks just as beautiful, if not more so, as the day she walked back into my life all those years ago.

"You're smoking," she says softly.

"Yeah, sorry." I put the cigarette out in the bowl, pushing it aside with my foot.

"Don't be sorry. If I smoked, I'd be having one right now." She looks down at her bare feet, curling her toes in, as she runs her hands down her skirt.

It makes me want to touch her. I need to touch her.

Her eyes lift back to mine, and the ache in them hurts me. "I'm sorry I left earlier. I know I should have stayed and talked. I was just…"

"Angry."

"Yeah." She blows out a breath.

She's still standing in the doorway. Too far away.

I need her here.

"Come here." There's no argument in my tone.

And there's no argument from her as she pads toward.

She goes to sit beside me, but I pull her onto my lap. With her legs on either side of my thighs, I band my arms around her waist. Burying my face into her chest, I just breathe her in.

The feel of her along with her scent always calm everything around me.

"I want to be angry," she says quietly. But her hands tell me different words as her fingers gently sift through my hair. "But I just kept thinking about you—when you were a kid…and your dad…and if you hadn't had us…"

I tip my head back, staring into her eyes. They're glazed with the past and the present. The sight brings up memories of things I haven't thought of in a long time. And I hate that she's thinking of them now, that this is making her think, making her hurt.

If Tru hurts, I hurt. We're bound together.

She's the other half of me.

The best half of me.

"I don't want this boy to be yours." Her voice catches, and tears creep in her eyes. "But the mother in me…I keep thinking, if it were JJ, Billy, or Belle…I just can't bear the thought of a child being alone without his mother. And…" She moistens her dry lips with her tongue. "Whatever happens, Jake, I'm right by your side. I'm *always* by your side."

And fuck if I don't love her more than I have in all the years combined in this moment.

"What did I do to deserve you?" My voice is hoarse, and the lump in my throat is the size of Texas.

"You just got lucky, I guess." Lifting her shoulders, she gives me a gentle teasing smile.

I press my lips to hers, reverently kissing her, like she deserves to be kissed, how she should always be kissed. I know she deserves better than me, but I'm selfish and I want her. I just pray to God that she doesn't wake up one day and realize this.

"You taste like the past," she murmurs against my lips.

I don't know if that's a good thing or a bad thing, and right now, I'm afraid to ask. Then, her grip on my hair tightens, and her thighs clamp around mine. She kisses me harder, and I know it's a good thing.

When she parts from my lips, I'm hard, and I want to be inside her. No matter what's happening or going on in our lives, I always want her. Nothing eases my mind or body like being buried deep inside Tru.

She places her hands against my cheeks, locking eyes with me. "I know I'm not perfect."

"I think you're pretty fucking perfect."

A small smile touches her lips as she gently shakes her head.

"I'm going to feel cheated that JJ...that he isn't your firstborn child. I might want to shout and scream, and I might hate the thought of how this will affect our kids, but I'm going to do my best to hold back my feelings and find a way for us to get through this. So, what I'm trying to say is...I know this isn't going to be easy, Jake, and I might feel hurt and angry if this boy is yours—"

"He's not mine."

She pauses, giving me a look. "You can't be sure of that."

"Yeah, I can."

"Nothing in this life is a surety, Jake."

"The way I feel about you is. I've loved you my whole life, Tru. There hasn't been a single second in it when I haven't loved you, and I'll continue to love you until my fucking black soul is dragged from this earth, kicking and screaming to hell. Then, I'll continue to love you from there."

"Your soul is not black. And you're not going to hell." There's a touch of laughter in her voice.

Knowing I've eased her hurt, even for a split second, has me feeling worthy of her—even if just for that split second.

"Well, I sure as fuck ain't going to heaven, sweetheart. Look..." I take ahold of her hand, pressing my lips to the palm, sliding my fingers between hers. I hold it against my face and stare deep into her eyes.

Looking into Tru's eyes wrecks me, but it's a wreckage I would happily go down with. I will go anywhere with her, do anything for her.

"I know you're trying to look at all the angles so you can ready yourself for this. But I'm telling you, there's nothing to ready yourself for. That kid isn't mine." I express the confidence in my words through my eyes to hammer the point home.

She gazes at me for a long moment. Then, closing her eyes on a blink, she releases a soft sigh. "You want him to be Jonny's. That's why you're so adamant that he's not yours."

Fuck.

Tru always can see right through me.

She's staring at me, and now, I can't bring myself to look at her.

So, I look past her, at the City of Angels spread out behind her.

"Is that wrong?" I whisper the words.

26

She runs her thumb over my cheek. "No. It's understandable. But, Jake...you...*we* need to prepare ourselves for the fact that he could be yours."

Releasing her hand, I press my face into the hollow of her neck, my hands sliding up her back to bring her as close to me as I can. Even then, it's not close enough.

I need more. I will always need more when it comes to her.

And I stay there, silent, breathing against her skin, inhaling her sweet scent.

No matter how much I might want to say it over and over again, telling her there's no chance that he's mine, she's right.

There is that slim possibility that he could be mine.

And, honestly, I don't know what the fuck to do with that.

FIVE

I watch Tru sleeping beside me.

The house is quiet, empty of the kids.

We should be tearing this place up, having crazy fucking sex in every room, like we used to before the kids came along.

Instead, I'm lying here, running all the what-ifs through my mind. Going over my past, I'm trying to remember this Tiffany chick who could potentially be the mother of my child. Pent-up aggression and frustration flow through me.

"Can't sleep?" Tru's soft voice surprises me.

"I thought you were sleeping."

"Trying to—unsuccessfully. I can hear the wheels turning in your mind. You wanna talk some more?"

Talk is all we've done

Talk and then have bouts of silence until neither of us could bear it. Then, when Tru suggested going to bed, I nearly sighed with relief.

I never thought we'd be here, that this would be us.

It's not us. Tru and I don't do this.

We don't dwell. We get on with things.

Namely, I want to get on with her.

"No, I don't want to talk." I roll over, putting myself on top of her. "I just want to feel…I *need* to feel *you*." I slide my hand up her waist, and wasting no time, I crush my mouth to hers.

And she's right there with me. Her arms wrap around my neck, and her legs come up and around my waist. She moans into my mouth, and I feel it all the way down to my cock.

"Fuck, I need you," I groan into her mouth.

"I know. I need you, too."

This isn't going to be slow loving. This is going to be hard and fast—but not too fast. It's been way too long since I've been inside my wife. I'm going to savor every fucking second of this.

Tru's hands work down my back, her fingers creeping into the waistband of my pajama bottoms.

Why the fuck am I wearing pajama bottoms when the kids aren't home? For that matter, why the hell is Tru wearing pajamas? They need to go now.

"Clothes off. Now," I tell her as I sit up.

I grab her pajama shorts and yank them off along with her panties, too, and then I attack her pajama top with the same ferocity.

Now, she's naked, just how I like her.

Fucking perfection.

"You still have clothes on." She gives me a sexy smile, nudging my pajama pants and massive boner with her toes.

I grab her foot and bring it up to my mouth. I run my tongue up her arch, loving the way she moans and lifts her back off the bed.

I nip her big toe with my teeth, making her squirm. Keeping hold of her foot, I shuck my pajama pants off. Then, I kiss my way up her gorgeous leg to her thigh. Her scent hits me, and my mouth starts to water.

I run my nose up her pussy, inhaling deeply. Then, I lift my eyes to hers. "I want you sitting on my face."

"And I want you in my mouth."

"Quite the dilemma." I grin at her. "But we can make it work."

I lie back on the bed next to Tru, and a beat later, she is on her knees, shifting around, until her beautiful ass is sitting just above my head.

I look up at her. Slightly bending over, she's already staring at me with needful eyes. Lust and want burn through me.

I reach up and grab ahold of her thighs, and I pull her straight onto my mouth. As my tongue plunges deep inside her, she falls forward on a gasp, her hands landing on my stomach.

This is exactly what we both need right now.

We need each other. We need to fuck each other, long and hard.

Just for tonight, we need to forget everything else and remember each other.

As long as I have her, then everything else will be okay.

She presses a kiss to my stomach. Her long hair brushes over my stomach and then my cock as she moves lower. Then, the next thing I feel is the silk of her tongue as she licks down the length of my cock from tip to root.

"Fuck," I moan against her pussy, my hips pushing up. I want more, need more.

I feel her hand wrap around the base of my cock. Then, her hot, wet mouth engulfs my cock, and she takes me in one long, hard suck that has my eyes rolling back in my head.

Sweet Jesus.

My wife gives the best blow jobs.

I momentarily lose concentration on what I was doing. Momentarily. This is me we're talking about.

Minutes later, Tru is coming apart under my mouth. And with the way her mouth has been working my cock, I'm not far behind her.

She starts to move off me, her mouth still on me. I grab ahold of her, my arm around her waist. My cock comes out of her mouth with a pop.

Keeping hold of Tru, I get up on my knees, putting her on all fours. I knee her legs apart. Then, I push my cock deep inside her.

"Fuck…" I groan. And I get high off the sound of her lustful moan, knowing how much she wants and needs me.

Reaching out, I gather her hair, wrapping it around my hand. With my other hand gripping her hip, I start fucking her.

"Jake…" My name slips from her lips sounding breathy and needy.

"Talk dirty to me, babe."

She groans and then says, "*Dame mas duro*, Jake! *Dame lo que yo necesito.*"

Those words from her, and I'm undone.

I know exactly what that means. Being with Tru all these years, I've picked up on a few things and meanings, especially the dirty words. And nothing does it for me like her telling me in her native tongue to fuck her harder and give her what she wants.

And that's just what I do. I pound into her, hard, exactly like we both need.

THE STORM

"Fuck, Jake! I'm...coming!" she cries out, her pussy quickly convulsing around my cock, squeezing me hard.

But I'm nowhere near done.

I flip Tru over onto her back and push inside her. Dipping my head, I take her nipple into my mouth, laving it with my tongue.

I fucking love Tru's body. I will never get enough of her.

Her fingers tangle in my hair, and she pulls my mouth up to hers. Her tongue slips into my mouth, and I lose my damn mind. Grabbing her hands, I pin them to the bed, and I start fucking her like a madman.

With the sound of wet flesh slapping wet flesh and the feel of her tongue in my mouth, her fingers gripping mine, her legs wrapped around me, I'm coming hard. I always come hard with Tru.

"Fuck...I'm coming, babe. I'm fucking...coming!"

I press my forehead against her cheek as I ride my orgasm out in her, filling her with all I have.

She moves her head a little, and presses a kiss to my hair. "You okay?" She sounds breathless.

My own breaths are out of control. My heart is pounding.

I lift my head and stare down at her. "I'm fine. I'm better than fine. I'm amazing. You okay? I was rough with you."

I let go of her hands. Resting down on my elbow, supporting my weight, I smooth her hair off her face.

"You're always rough with me." She smiles. "And I love it."

"I love that you love it." I grin before brushing my lips over hers.

"I don't want to move," she says.

"Why would we move?" I tip my head back, looking in her eyes. "The kids are at your parents. I see no reason to move."

33

"We need to clean up."

I shake my head at her.

"No?" she says.

"No," I echo.

My cock is still inside her and semi-hard. I pull out a little and then push back inside.

She lets out a gasp, lust glazing her eyes. "You not done?" she breathes.

Leaning close, I nip her lower lip with my teeth. "I haven't even fucking started."

SIX

I took the DNA test a few days ago. A swab in my mouth—that was all it was.

The results are due back today.

Bob, Jonny's dad, did his DNA test the same day I did. He's Jonny's only living relative. Jonny's mom, Lyn, died two years ago. She had a stroke and never recovered.

I briefly spoke to Bob the other day. There wasn't a lot we could say. I know he wants Storm to be Jonny's. Fuck, so do I.

But there is the chance he could be mine.

And not to sound derogatory against Tiffany, but there's also the chance that Storm is neither Jonny's or mine.

Both Tru and I are at home today. There was no way I could go into the label today. And Tru didn't want to go to work. She wanted to be here when the call came in.

JJ and Billy are at school. Belle is spending the day with Tru's mom and dad.

Tru and I are shielding the kids from this. We haven't told them anything, but they know something's going on. They're smart kids.

Stuart has kept it out of the press so far. The bare minimum of people knows. Besides Stuart and Jerry—my lawyer—Bob and his lawyer, Eva and Billy, and Simone know, but Denny doesn't know. Tru swore Simone to secrecy.

I don't want Denny or Tom to know yet—not until I know either way.

I don't want them getting their hopes up that Storm might be Jonny's son because I know they would.

I know because it's what I would want—*do* want.

I'm sitting at the breakfast bar, nursing a lukewarm cup of coffee, pretending to read some papers that Stuart sent over yesterday for a new band we're signing. The TV is on low in the background, filling the silence.

Tru is cleaning. She's been at it since first thing this morning. There's no need for her to clean because we have a cleaner, but I know she's doing it to keep busy. So far, she's emptied the cupboards out and cleaned them. Then, she cleaned the fridge. Now, she's wiping down surfaces and cupboard doors.

I think she's running out of things to clean.

I'm just hoping this fucking call comes in soon.

I get up from my stool and take my coffee to the sink. After pouring it out, I rinse the cup and put it in the dishwasher.

Then, I walk over to Tru. I turn her around, pull her close, and wrap my arms around her. She sinks into my body, her arms coming around my waist.

I press my lips to the top of her head. "It's going to be okay," I say softly.

She releases a breath against my chest and gently nods her head.

My cell starts to ring on the breakfast bar. Tru's body tenses in my arms. She lifts her head and stares up at me.

This is it.

I can see the fear in her eyes, and it elevates my own.

I'm sure that Storm isn't mine. But Tru's worries make my own heighten.

I kiss her forehead. Then, I walk over to the breakfast bar and pick up my cell, glancing at the screen.

"It's my lawyer," I tell Tru.

My heart sets off beating like a motherfucker, and my hand trembles. I can feel myself starting to waver.

I turn to her. "Tru…"

She meets my stare, hers steely with determination and looking a hell of a lot stronger than they did a moment ago.

But that's Tru. When I can't be strong, she is for the both of us.

"We'll be fine, Jake," she tells me. "Just answer the call."

My chest lifts on a breath.

Taking a step back, I let my ass hit a breakfast stool as I connect the call, putting my cell to my ear. "Jerry."

Tru comes and sits on the stool beside mine. I turn in my seat to face her, and I take her hand in mine.

"Jake, hi. Look, I won't beat around the bush, as I know how important this is to you and Tru. Storm…he isn't yours."

I blow out an audible breath, all tension dropping from my body. "I knew it."

From my response, Tru knows the result. I see the relief spread from her eyes to across her face.

I bring her hand to my mouth, and I kiss it.

The next thought in my mind is, *Is he Jonny's?*

I know Jerry won't know the answer to that question, so I don't bother asking.

"Thanks, Jerry. I appreciate you calling."

I hang up my cell, dropping it back on the counter.

A second later, Tru has her arms around me, her face buried in my neck. I can feel her relief rolling off of her in waves. I wrap my arms around her, holding her tight.

"He's not mine," I say the words out loud. It's like I'm taking my first breath in days.

She squeezes me tighter. I hold her harder.

"I'm sorry I put you through this," I say, pressing a kiss to her hair.

She moves back a touch, staring into my eyes. "You didn't put me through this, Jake. It wasn't something you knowingly did. It was your past that came back to try to hurt us. I accepted your past and that possibility a long time ago, Jake. You have nothing to be sorry for." She brushes her fingers over my cheek. "I know how hard these last few days have been on you. And I'm proud of you and how strong you've been."

I know what she's saying. She's proud of me because I didn't fall back on old habits to get me through this.

I never would have. I have too much to lose.

"I smoked," I tell her. "A lot." More than she knows about.

"What's a lot?"

"Two cartons." I grimace.

The corner of her lip lifts. "I can see past the cigarettes—so long as they're not a permanent fixture."

"They're not, but I might need some nicotine patches for the next week."

I grin, and she laughs.

And I fucking love the sound. I've hated not hearing her laugh during these past few days. The house sounded so quiet without her joy filling it.

The smile on her face quickly disappears, and her gaze dips. "Jake…I'm happy that Storm isn't yours. Does that make me a bad person?" She bites her lower lip. "I mean, his mother is dying, and he's going to be all alone. For my own selfish reasons, I'm relieved that he's not your son, and—"

"Stop it. It doesn't make you bad. It makes you human, sweetheart." I cup her cheek with my hand, forcing her eyes up to mine. "I'm relieved, too."

She stares at me for a long moment. Then, she leans in close and softly kisses me. "So…does this mean that he's Jonny's?"

I blow out a breath, running a hand through my hair. "I don't know, babe." I meet her eyes again. "But I need to know."

"Call Bob, and find out," she tells me.

Tru goes to move back to her stool, but I stop her with my arm around her waist, holding her there. I need her close, for whichever way this call goes.

I pick up my cell and dial Bob's number.

It rings for a long while. My stomach is churning, my heart pounding the whole time.

"Jake?" Bob's voice comes down the line. It sounds unsteady, almost like he's been crying.

Fuck.

My heart beats even harder. I feel like it's going to come out of my ribs. I'm more anxious for his results than I was for my own.

"Yeah, it's me. I-I got my results. Storm…he's not mine. Do you…do you have your results back?"

"Yeah. My lawyer called a few minutes ago. Jake, he's…" His voice catches and breaks.

My stomach bottoms out.

"Bob?"

"He's Jonny's. He's Jonny's son."

He's Jonny's son.

I have...I have Jonny back—well, a part of him at least.

Then, something happens to me that hasn't happened in a very long time.

I start to cry.

SEVEN

"Jonny has a son?"

The disbelief in Tom's voice mirrors the look on Denny's face. And it resonates the sound my own voice had this morning.

"Yeah, man, he does." I nod.

"I...Jesus Christ." Tom's voice breaks.

"How did you find out? When did you find out?" Denny cuts in, taking the heat off an obviously struggling Tom.

"I found out this morning that he is Jonny's son. A few days ago, a lawyer contacted Stuart about a paternity suit against me and also Jonny. The mom's a groupie from back in the early days. She wasn't sure if the father was Jonny or me. I did a DNA test, and so did Jonny's dad. We got the results a few hours ago."

"This was why Tru was all upset and pissed off when she came around to see Simone the other day?"

"Yeah."

"Fuck," Denny breathes out.

"What's his name?" Tom asks me. His voice is off, sounding exactly like I did when I found out that he was Jonny's.

"Storm."

"Good name." Denny gives me a knowing look.

"How old is he?" That's Tom again.

"Thirteen."

"When can we meet him?"

"I'm flying out to New York tomorrow to see Bob. Then, I'm taking him to meet Storm. I guess…we can arrange for something after that. We just have to take this one slowly."

Tipping his head back, Tom presses the heels of his hands to his eyes, rubbing at them.

This has hit him hard—about as hard as it hit me. Denny is struggling, too. He's just always been able to handle shit better than Tom and I can.

"You doing okay?" I reach over and squeeze Tom's shoulder.

"Yeah." He drops his hands, blowing out a breath. "I just—fuck. It's just surreal, you know? I mean, I know Jonny's gone, but it's like getting a part of him back."

"I know, man." I give his shoulder one last squeeze and then remove my hand.

"Does he look like Jonny?" Tom asks.

"I don't know." I shake my head. "I haven't seen a picture of him."

"Why now?" Denny pipes up. "Why is the mother just coming forward now? Does she want money?"

My eyes meet with Denny's. "She's dying."

"Jesus fucking Christ," Denny exhales.

"Yeah." I know what he's thinking. Storm's mother is dying, and now, he's going to find out that his father is already dead.

"She's the only family he has...well, had," I add.

"Damn fucking right, had. He has us now. We're his family." Tom slams his hand down on the table.

"Will Storm live with Bob?" Denny asks me.

"Honestly, I don't know. Everything has happened so fast. I just don't know. And it's not that Bob wouldn't want him 'cause I know he would, but he's old, and he's not well. I don't know if he could take on a teenager."

"Then, he'll come and live with one of us."

My eyes go to Tom—not in surprise, but because he's spoken the words that have been circling around in my mind since I found out Storm was Jonny's.

"We're not leaving Jonny's kid to fend for himself," Tom says, "or to have him end up in some goddamn foster home. No fucking way. He's Jonny's kid, and that makes him ours, too. Jonny would have wanted us to look after him. You know he would have."

"I know, man. And we will. You're not saying anything I haven't been thinking myself."

"Then, what do we do?" Denny asks. "This kid doesn't know us. He's about to lose his mother. He's gonna be struggling. And him coming to live with a bunch of strange people...it's not gonna be easy on him."

Denny is always the voice of reason.

"None of this is gonna be easy for him. Unfortunately, he doesn't have the luxury of choice. Honestly, I don't know what we can do." I blow out a breath. "We can't just charge in there like bulls and make demands or claims on him. But you are right. I guess...just let me go there

43

tomorrow with Bob and meet the mother and Storm, and then we'll go from there. Agreed?"

"Agreed," they say in unison.

EIGHT

"How you doing?" I glance over at Bob, who is sitting beside me in the backseat of the black Mercedes that Dave hired to drive us in while we're in New York.

We're on our way to Queens to meet Tiffany. Well, I say *meet*, but, apparently, I met her a long time ago. But this will be Bob's first time meeting her.

We don't get to meet Storm yet. He's at school at the moment. Tiffany wanted to speak to us before he gets home.

I get that. He's her kid. She'll want to protect him as best she can.

I'm itching to meet Storm. I want to know what he's like—if he's like Jonny, if he looks like his father, if he loves music. *Does he play the guitar like Jonny did?* I mean, it was in Jonny's blood. For Jonny, playing the guitar was as easy as breathing. *Did Storm inherit that?*

I have so many questions floating around in my head, questions that can only be answered from meeting Storm.

Bob and I haven't really talked about what's going to happen when it comes to Storm's living arrangements—not that we've had much time to talk. I flew from LA to New York, and then we picked up Bob from his house. Now, we're driving to Astoria in Queens where Tiffany and Storm live in an apartment above a bakery.

Tiffany is receiving in-house care, and her best friend is helping take care of Storm.

Bob turns his head from the window to look at me. "I'm okay." He shrugs. "I just…I wanna meet him, you know?"

"Yeah, I know," I breathe out the words.

"Thanks for coming with me, Jake."

I slide my eyes to him. "You don't have to thank me. I'd have come even if you didn't want me to."

I give him a small smile, and he chuckles.

Then, he turns his face forward and blows out a tired-sounding breath, linking his hands together. "I don't know what to do, Jake."

"'Bout what?"

He gives me a quick look before turning his eyes away. "Storm."

The one word tells me everything he's concerned about.

I knew Bob was sick. His heart is weak, and he's old.

He's aged so much since Lyn passed.

When I saw him half an hour ago, for the first time in a year, I felt guilty. I should have been around for him more. It's easy to forget when I'm happy and busy with Tru and the kids. But seeing Bob now, I feel like I've failed Jonny again.

And it's going to stop now.

"You don't have to worry about anything or make any decisions right now. You just focus on meeting your grandson, and I'll take care of everything else."

He looks back to me, and I see the relief in his eyes.

Bob is a proud man, but he's also a realist. He might not have to worry about money, due to Jonny's trust, but taking care of a teenager is a whole other ball game.

And I pretty much have things worked out in my head. I just have to get everyone else to agree. I know I said to Denny and Tom that we needed to take this slowly, and I intend on doing that—well, kind of.

I've never been one to mess around. When I want something, I make sure it happens.

But this is delicate, and I have to consider other people—like my family, first and foremost.

Thankfully, I have the one person I need behind me— Tru. We sat down and talked last night before I left. Tru had known what I wanted to do before I even said it. I love that she just gets me. And I also love her for agreeing with my plan.

And my plan is to bring Jonny's kid home with me.

NINE

"We're here," Dave says from the front of the car as he brings us to a stop outside Marie's Country Bakery.

I start to feel something I haven't felt in a long time as I stare out the window at the bakery—nerves. Nerves are something I just don't do. But this is Jonny's kid. He's important.

The store is nice, and it's quiet from the looks of things.

I can see straight inside, thanks to the glass front, and I see shitloads of cakes and pastries.

Tru would be in heaven here. Maybe I should get something to take home for her and the kids.

First things first though…

I pull my ball cap and sunglasses from my jacket pockets and put them on. Right now is a time I could do without being recognized.

"You ready?" I ask Bob.

"As I'll ever be." He gives me a nod.

We all get out of the car at the same time. We don't hang about in the street. We head straight inside. A bell dings as I push open the door. Bob and Dave follow behind me.

A red-haired woman is standing behind the counter with a smile on her face, but it quickly fades.

It's not the usual response I get from women.

I'm guessing that she's Marie. And I'm also guessing that she's realized who we are.

Why she has any reason to be unhappy with us, I have no clue.

If anyone should be unhappy, it's Bob. He's missed out on thirteen years of his grandson's life.

Then again, her best friend is dying. I can't see that I would have a lot to be happy about, if it were me.

"I'm Jake Wethers," I say as I step up to the counter. "And this is Bob Creed. We're here to see Tiffany."

"I know who you are." She stares at me for a long moment. Then, she nods in the direction of my ball cap and sunglasses, as if telling me it's an ineffective disguise.

I pull the cap and sunglasses off, putting them back in my pocket.

"I'm Marie, Tiffany's best friend. Tiffany's upstairs. Just let me close the shop, and I'll take you upstairs to her."

We stand and wait while she comes out from behind the counter. She turns the *Closed* sign on the door and locks up.

"Follow me," she says—well, more like orders.

Taking a deep breath, I usher Bob to go first, and we all silently follow Marie into the back of the shop, then through a door, and up a flight of stairs.

When we reach the small landing at the top of the stairs, Marie opens the door, taking us into the hallway of what I'm guessing is Tiffany and Storm's apartment.

"I'll wait out here," Dave tells me, taking up his position on the landing outside the door.

I give him a nod before Marie closes the door on him.

She turns to face Bob and me. "Tiffany is in the living room," she says in a hushed tone. "Don't do *anything* to upset her."

I part my lips to speak, but Bob beats me to it.

"We're not here to upset Tiffany, Marie. We're just here to talk about my grandson," Bob tells her in a gentle manner while I grit my teeth.

She looks at Bob and then me. For some reason, her eyes narrow on me.

What the fuck have I done?

Then, she looks back to Bob, and her face relaxes a little. "I'll take you through," she says to Bob in a tone sounding a little nicer than before.

We walk down the hall and into a small living room. And on a chair by the window is Tiffany.

"Tiffany, Bob and Jake are here to see you."

She looks straight at me. I see the familiarity come to life in her eyes, but I know it's not in mine because I don't recognize her.

It's been years—I know it has—and of course, she wouldn't look the same. I can see that the cancer has ravaged her body. She looks frail. And I assume the headscarf she's wearing is to cover the loss of her hair.

If I'm being totally honest, I didn't think I would recognize her. But a part of me hoped I would, so I could tell myself that my life wasn't as fucked up as I remembered it to be.

Clearly, it was.

I force myself to smile at her. I know it's as awkward as I feel.

"You don't remember me, do you?" There's no malice or distaste in her tone. She's just plainly stating a fact.

"I don't. I'm sorry." I shake my head.

"Don't be sorry." She smiles. "You lived a different life back then."

Her eyes move from me to Bob. "Mr. Creed." She smiles as she puts down the book in her hand on the small table by her chair, and she starts to slowly get up.

"Don't get up," Bob says, stopping her, as he walks over to her. Leaning down, he takes her hand. "Thank you," he says to her in earnest, "for giving me a part of my Jonny back."

Fuck.

I can't stop the blur in my eyes or the burn in the back of my throat.

Irrespective of everything, the fact that she kept Storm hidden from us for thirteen years doesn't matter because, now, we have something we never dreamed we could have.

Pressing my hands to my hips, I look to the floor, blowing out a breath.

Marie is quiet behind me.

"I don't deserve your thanks, Mr. Creed—"

"Please call me Bob."

"Bob, I kept Storm from you for thirteen years. You have a right to be angry about that."

"None of that matters now. And I know you must have had your reasons. My Jonny…he was easy to love, hard to handle."

Fuck. This hurts to hear.

I pinch the bridge of my nose, exhaling another breath.

"I know the way Jonny lived his life. He and Jake both."

My name brings my eyes to them, but neither of them is looking at me.

"Tom and Denny, too. And if you took on one of those boys, you took them all on. They always were a package deal. And I can understand not wanting to raise a baby around the kind of lifestyle they all lived back then. They were pretty wild."

She lets out a relieved-sounding laugh. "Yeah, I guess I was a little wild back then, too—before Storm was born. I changed the minute I found out I was pregnant."

Bob rubs a hand on his back, and I can see that he's struggling with standing.

"Let me get you a chair, Bob." I get an armchair and pull it over, opposite Tiffany's chair, so Bob can sit. I take a seat on the edge of the sofa adjacent to them.

"Marie, you can get back to the shop. I'll be okay here."

Marie gives her a dubious look. "You sure?"

For fuck's sake, what does she think we're going to do to Tiffany?

"I'm sure." Tiffany smiles.

"You want me to make some tea before I go?"

"Do you want anything to drink?" Tiffany asks Bob and me.

"I could drink a tea," Bob says.

"Jake?" Tiffany looks at me.

"I'm fine," I say.

"Tea for me and Bob would be great. Thanks, Marie."

Tiffany watches Marie leave the room.

Then, she looks at Bob and me. "So, I'm sure you've got questions for me."

"Look, I don't want to be the asshole here, and at the risk of sounding like one, I'm going to get straight to the point. Obviously, you've come to us now because you need help with Storm. Without a doubt, that will happen. But I want to know how you see this playing out," I say.

Bob gives me an annoyed look. But I don't regret my words. It's best to get this out of the way. Then, I'll ask everything I can about the kid.

She stares at me for a moment. "I'm Storm's only family. Honestly, I haven't properly thought this through. I just know I'm running out of time."

"We don't need to talk about this now," Bob cuts in. "This is a conversation for another day. Right now, I just want to know all there is to know about my grandson."

Marie comes back with the tea, so I clamp my lips shut and let Bob ask his questions about Storm.

I listen intently for the next half an hour as Tiffany tells us about Storm's life—how good his grades are in school and that he has some behavioral issues. But she skirts around that, glossing over details like any good mother would.

He likes music. That makes me happy. He plays guitar. That makes me even happier.

He's Jonny kid for sure. The more she talks about Storm, the more I hear Jonny in her words.

I've stayed silent with my own questions for long enough, and now, I have to ask them. It might anger Bob, but I need to know. "Tiffany, I have to know…why didn't you come to us when you found out you were pregnant? We could have helped. Jonny could have known his son."

"Things were wild back then. We were all doing drugs and each other. It wasn't a decision I came to lightly. Back then, I was in love with Jonny. Jake, you and I…" She looks away. "Well, I was with Jonny, too, and over that time, I fell in love. But I wasn't his only. I wasn't stupid enough to think I was or ever would be."

"That might be, but he would have cared for his son."

"Maybe you're right. But back then, I couldn't take that risk. When I found out I was pregnant, I didn't know if the baby was yours or Jonny's. God, I was so scared. My parents were deeply religious. I was already a huge disappointment, an embarrassment, to them. I didn't know what to do. So…" She blows out a breath. "I decided to tell Jonny. No offense, Jake, but Jonny was always so much more approachable than you. He was less…intense, I guess. So, after I plucked up the courage to go see him, I went to your place in New York. There was a party happening, like usual. You weren't there. Neither was Tom or Denny—that I saw. I looked around for Jonny. I finally found him in his bedroom…" She turns her eyes to Bob. "I'm so sorry to be saying these things about your son in front of you."

"Don't be. There's nothing you could say that would shock me, Tiffany. I knew my son, and I loved him all the same."

She exhales slowly and looks back at me. "I went into his room. He was passed out on his bed…with a belt strapped around his arm and a used needle on the bed beside him. A couple of girls were passed out in the room—one on the bed, one on the floor. Cocaine was on the nightstand. Empty bottles of alcohol were everywhere. Nothing I hadn't seen before, but being pregnant made me see it through clearer eyes. In that moment, I knew that I couldn't bring a baby into that lifestyle. If I'd told Jonny I was pregnant, that's exactly what would have happened."

I knew those things about Jonny. I knew he'd injected from time to time. I never used the needle, but he had. I hated that he had, but I never tried to stop him. I was always high. What kind of hypocrite would I have been when I was barely sober for a day?

"My parents disowned me when I told them I wouldn't give the baby up," Tiffany continues. "So, I moved away from New York. I got a cheap condo in Queens. It was a struggle. I managed on welfare until Storm was a year old, and then I got a job working at Marie's bakery. The job came with a room in the apartment above it. We've been here ever since. And we've been happy—until…I got sick, that is."

SAMANTHA TOWLE

I'm just about to ask her about her illness. How long does she have left? What's going to happen to Storm when she's gone?

But then I hear voices, and the front door opens and slams shut.

Tiffany's eyes flash to the clock on the wall. "He's home early," she says.

"Did he know we'd be here?" I ask.

"Yes. He knew you were coming to see him. But I was expecting him at three thirty. He's early, which means he left school an hour before he was supposed to, and that means he's in trouble."

"What exactly does he know about this situation?" I ask quietly, not believing I didn't already ask this. "Does he know that I could have been…"

Tiffany shakes her head. "No. He knows there were two men…who could have potentially been his father," she says the words quietly. "He knows about Jonny now, but he doesn't know that you were the other man in the equation."

Pulling my eyes from Tiffany, I stare at the open doorway, listening to the heavy footsteps in the hallway, my heart beating in double time.

Then, a second later, Jonny's double appears in the doorway, and my heart goes into free fall.

TEN

I'm staring.

I know I'm staring.

But I feel like I'm back in the past. Every inch of Storm is Jonny. It's terrifying and amazing at the same time.

Looking at Storm is like looking at Jonny the first time I met him when I moved to the States.

Storm is Jonny's exact double—from his lean frame to the shagginess of his long dirty-blond hair that he keeps brushing out of his blue eyes...Jonny's eyes. And they are staring straight back at me.

If there were any lingering doubts that Storm wasn't Jonny's, that disappeared the moment I laid eyes on him.

"Storm, what are you doing home early?" Tiffany's gentle voice carries across the room.

Storm moves his stare from me to Bob. Finally, his eyes go to his mother. "I had a free period," he finally answers.

Jesus. He even sounds like Jonny.

I don't know whether to cry in relief or pain.

Tiffany gives Storm the same look that Tru gives to Billy when he's been in trouble at school, which isn't often. He just has a little of my naughty in him.

Tiffany doesn't question Storm on it, seemingly letting it go.

I get to my feet. Pressing my clammy hands against my jeans, I clear my throat. "Storm…I'm Jake."

He looks at me again. His stare jolts through me. I can't get a read on him. His eyes are closed off.

"I know who you are."

Of course he does.

"Storm…" Bob's voice comes from behind me, a shake to it.

I glance at Bob as he moves forward, standing beside me.

"I'm Bob. I'm your…grandfather. It's so wonderful to meet you."

Storm says nothing. He just stands there, staring at both of us.

Then, his expression seems to shut down. He takes a step back, retreating.

Something yanks inside me. It feels a lot like fear and loss.

The feeling intensifies when he turns to leave.

"Storm." Tiffany's voice carries a commanding tone, causing him to stop.

He glances back over his shoulder at her.

"Where are you going?"

Her looks at us again and then away to the floor. "My room," he says low but with hardness.

It's a tone I heard Jonny use many times.

I hear the creak of a chair and look to see Tiffany getting to her feet.

"Bob and Jake came a long way to see you."

"Am I supposed to be grateful?" His voice takes on an edge.

"Storm," Tiffany snaps.

"No. This is bullshit. It's all bullshit!"

"Storm! Stop this right now."

He glares at his mother. I can feel his anger emanating from him, and I understand where it's coming from.

I also realize this is going to be a lot harder than I anticipated.

But that doesn't mean I'm changing my mind—not now, not when I have Jonny's flesh and blood standing in front of me.

"You will stay here and get to know your grandfather and your father's closest friend."

His eyes narrow on me, and I can see something resembling blame.

Then, his stare flickers to his mother. "But that's just the thing, isn't it? I don't have a father. He's dead, remember?" He bites out each word, and then the living room door slams shut behind him as he leaves, shaking the room.

I hear another door slam quickly after, and I guess that's his bedroom door.

"I'm so sorry." Tiffany comes over to Bob. "He's not normally like this. He's such a sweet boy. He's just…he's been struggling since I was…since my prognosis. Then, he found out about his father…who he is—*was*…that he's…gone."

"There's no need to apologize." Bob puts his hand on her arm. "What do you want us to do? Should we leave?"

Fuck no, I don't want to leave. I want to go into that room and demand that kid to talk to me.

Tiffany's eyes move to the door. She lets out a sigh. "Maybe that's best for now. Let me talk to him. Then, you can come back later and have dinner with us."

ELEVEN

Can't say I liked the fact that we had to leave Tiffany and Storm's apartment. The stubbornness in me wanted to demand that we stay and talk to him.

Leaving felt like leaving Jonny. I know that's stupid.

But losing Jonny...and then finding out a piece of him is still here...

Storm is the closest thing I've got to Jonny. I'm not letting that go for anything.

Jonny would have wanted me to be there for Storm, to do what he himself couldn't, to help Storm.

But the father in me knew that demanding to stay, forcing Storm to talk to me, wouldn't have worked.

So, I swallowed my pride and left with Bob, promising that we'd return at seven thirty to have dinner with Storm and Tiffany.

The drive back to Bob's house is quiet.

I know Bob must be feeling as disappointed as I am about not getting any time with Storm.

But it's not just that.

It was seeing the kid himself for the first time—how much he is like Jonny and not just in looks but also personality, the spit and fire in him. That is Jonny.

I know Storm isn't Jonny. But in that moment…it was like Jonny was back here, standing in that living room with us.

I hear Bob exhale, pulling my eyes to him. He's staring out the car window.

"Standing in that living room with Storm…I felt like I'd been thrown back twenty years, and Jonny was right there in front of me." Bob's voice is uneven.

Thinking about how hard this is for me, I can't even imagine how hard it must be for Bob. If I'd lost JJ, Billy, or Belle…I can't even consider it. It would destroy me. I'd never recover.

"He's Jonny," I softly say the words.

Bob's eyes come to mine. He looks tired, weary. It makes me worry.

"Yeah," he exhales. "But that's just it, Jake. He's not Jonny. No matter how much he looks like Jonny, sounds like him…how much we might miss Jonny and want him back, Storm isn't him. He's his own person…a kid who's about to lose his mother. And he's just found out that his father is also dead. We need to push our own feelings aside in this. We need to think about him and what's best for him."

"And what do you think is best for him? Because I think being with his family is what will be best for him."

Regret fills his eyes, and he looks away from me, his hands gripping his knees. "You know, I always felt like I'd missed the mark with Jonny."

I reach over and put my hand on Bob's shoulder, giving it a squeeze, before letting go. "You were a great dad, Bob. Trust me, I know bad ones, and you most definitely weren't a bad dad."

"Yeah, I did everything right. I went to all his school plays, watched his gigs, supported him. But there was always something missing, something inside of him that I could never reach, something angry and unfulfilled. I should have done more to stop the drugs…with all of you."

His eyes come back to me.

"There was nothing you could have done. We all had to find our own way. Jonny's death was not your fault," I tell him.

His eyes glaze with tears, and it hurts me to see him in pain.

"It was my fault because I'm his dad. And it was my job to protect him…protect him from the world and himself. I failed at that. I don't want to fail again with Storm. He needs me now. He'll need me more when Tiffany dies. He's going to need me. I'm his family."

"*We* are his family."

Gratitude fills his eyes. "I'm man enough to admit that taking care of him, without Lyn here, terrifies me, Jake. I don't want to fail that boy. I *can't* fail him."

I shift in my seat, turning to him. "You won't fail him because you're not doing this alone. I wanted to wait and see exactly what it is that Tiffany wants from us for Storm before speaking to you about this. I don't know if she has a plan in her mind for his care when she's gone. But as far as I'm concerned, whatever she does have in mind, if it doesn't involve us, then we'll change that.

"I spoke to Tru before I left to come here, and she agrees with me. I'm hoping that you will, too. We want you and Storm to come to LA and live with us. You could either move into the house with us, or Stuart's old place on our property is empty. But we want you close by. We want Storm with us. And it'd ease the burden of you raising him alone."

I prepare myself for Bob to reject my offer. I know I'm asking for a lot. I'm asking for him to leave his home, his city. And Bob is a proud man. I'm just hoping that, with age, he's gotten realistic.

He glances away. For a few long seconds, he looks out the window at New York moving past us. Then, his eyes come back to me. "A change of scenery might be just what Storm and I both need."

A smile pushes up my lips, and I sit back in my seat. "We've just got to convince Tiffany now."

Bob huffs out a short laugh. "I don't think Tiffany is going to be the one we'll have to convince."

That, I have to agree on.

Storm might not be Jonny, but from what I saw earlier, he has his father's stubbornness. And one thing with Jonny was, once he'd set his mind on something, there was no changing it.

I just hope I can get Storm to my way of thinking.

If I've learned anything from my kids, it's that, if I want to get them to do something, I have to make them think it was their idea in the first place.

I just need to figure out how to do that with Storm.

TWELVE

When we get to Bob's house, I head straight upstairs to call Tru. Dave and I are staying at Bob's tonight, at his insistence, rather than checking in at a hotel.

Lyn and Bob never moved, so this is the house Jonny grew up in. I remember Jonny offering to buy them a bigger place after the money started rolling in when our band hit the big time, but they turned him down.

Even now, Bob is a wealthy man from what Jonny left them, but he doesn't mirror his riches with how he lives.

I guess the money is something Bob will need to take into consideration, now that Jonny has an heir. I'll talk with him about that later.

Right now, I just want to talk to my wife and kids.

As I step into Jonny's old room, a hundred memories wash over me.

The room hasn't changed. It's still a shrine to Jonny's memory.

The posters of naked chicks and bands are on the walls. Jonny's old music sheets and his first ever guitar, his Fender Stratocaster, are propped up on a guitar stand. A mini guitar amp and guitar pedal are sitting on the floor next to it.

Even after all these years, I can still smell my youth in here with the lingering cigarette smoke and stench of grungy teenage boys who didn't realize that showering regularly would be a good start to getting girls.

It brings a sad smile to my lips.

I drop my bag on the floor and sit on the edge of the bed.

I stare over at a framed picture on the desk of Jonny, Tom, Denny, and me. It was taken right before we did our official first gig as The Mighty Storm. I remember shitting myself that night. Jonny was calm as fuck, like he just knew he was born to be up onstage.

Sucking in a breath, I shut my eyes.

"Why did you have to fucking die?" I breathe the words out. Opening my eyes, I focus in on him in the picture. "You should be here, Jon. You should be here with your kid."

Rubbing my eyes dry, I get my cell from my pocket and FaceTime Tru's cell. I need to see my family's beautiful faces as well as hear their voices right now.

"Hey, baby," she answers.

The sight of Tru's face and the sound of her soothing voice ease me.

"How are you doing?"

"I'm better now," I tell her with a smile.

She smiles back, lighting up her face. "How did it go with Storm?"

I let out a breath, my fingers rubbing my forehead. "Not great. He didn't want to talk to us. He stormed off to his bedroom. Tiffany suggested we go back later for dinner after she's had time to talk to him."

"Makes sense. He's thirteen and going through a lot right now. His emotions have got to be all over the place."

"Yeah, I just…"

"Patience, Jake. I know you don't have much of it, but you're gonna need it in spades with this kid."

"I'm trying." I give a weak smile that I know she totally doesn't buy.

"How's Bob doing?"

"He's holding up. I spoke to him about him and Storm moving in with us. He agrees it's the right thing. Just need to speak to Tiffany and Storm about it now."

"What's Storm like?"

"Exactly like Jonny." As I say the words, the emotions I've been holding in all day come out, my eyes filling with tears.

I don't have to pretend in front of Tru. She's the only one I can ever be myself with.

"It was like I went back in time, and I was thirteen years old with Jonny standing in front of me."

"Oh, honey," she whispers, touching her fingers to the screen.

I press my fingertips against hers on the small screen of my cell.

"It was just a shock, seeing him, you know?" I move my hand from the screen and dry my eyes on my sleeve.

"I know, baby. So…you're going back tonight for dinner?"

"Yeah. Hopefully, we can spend some time with Storm and talk to Tiffany about where we go from here."

"Is that Dad?"

I hear JJ's voice in the background.

Tru's head turns slightly. "Yeah. You wanna talk to him?"

The next thing I see is JJ's face.

"Hey, Dad. Guess what?" His brown eyes are all bright, and he has this huge smile on his face.

My heart feels lighter seeing him. He looks so much like Tru. Belle does, too. Only Billy has my black hair and blue eyes.

"What?" I smile.

"At school today, in recess, we were playing soccer— the boys from my class against the boys from the grade above us. We totally won! And the best thing? I scored the winning goal!"

"That's amazing, JJ!" I exclaim. "I wish I could have been there to see it."

"Yeah, me, too! It was so awesome, Dad. You would've loved it."

The next thing I hear is, "JJ! Where are you?"

The sound of Belle's squeaky voice makes me chuckle.

"I'm in Mom and Dad's room, talking to Dad," he tells her.

"Dada's home?"

"No, he's on the phone. You wanna talk to him?"

"Gimme phone."

The phone starts to move, and I'm guessing that Belle is grabbing at it.

JJ laughs. "Love you, Dad," he gets in before Belle wrestles the phone from him.

"Love you, too," I call out.

Then, I see Belle as she holds the phone up close to her face.

"Dada, guess what?"

"What?" I smile at her.

"I got mawwied today."

I freeze. "I'm sorry, what?"

"Mawwied. I got mawwied, Dada."

"Um...who to?"

"Cweed Cawter."

"Uncle Tom's Creed?"

"Uh-huh. Aunt Wywa, Cweed, and baby Woni came to pway. Aunt Mimone and her huge tummy and Fwankie came, too."

Tom and Lyla have two kids. Creed is the same age as Belle, and Joni is six months old. Simone and Denny just have Frankie at the moment—who's six, the same age as Billy—but Simone is pregnant with twins, and she's due in a few months.

And I'm going to be having some serious words with Tom, telling him to keep his kid in line. No way is my girl marrying a Carter—well, any male—ever. Belle's going to be a nun when she's older. I'm not even kidding.

"How exactly did you get married, Beauty?" I ask her.

She gives me a look that clearly says she thinks I'm stupid for not already knowing. "Dada, I held his hand, of cwouse."

I bite back the laughter wanting to burst from me. "And does Creed know that you're married, baby?"

She rolls her eyes at me. "Cwouse he does. I told him so."

Yep, she's definitely entering the nunnery when she's older.

I press my lips together, the tears in my eyes now from humor.

"I love you, Beauty."

"Wuv you, too, Dada. Bye." She kisses the screen, leaving wet lip marks on it.

Belle drops the phone, and the next thing I see through those lip marks is my bedroom ceiling.

"Um, Belle?" I call. "Tru? Anyone?"

"Hey." Tru's smiling face appears as she picks the up phone.

"Belle just dumped me and ran off," I tell her. "And she just told me about her marriage to Creed." I give Tru a look, raising my brow.

"Oh, yeah." Tru laughs. "No need to worry there. Poor Creed. He went white when she told him that they were married. He definitely doesn't have Tom's scent for women."

"Oh, give him time." I chuckle. "Where's Billy?"

"He's in his room, sulking." She looks like she's holding back a smile.

"Why's he sulking?"

"He got in trouble at school today."

My boys aren't bad boys, but it's not totally unusual for them to get into trouble from time to time. They have my naughty streak.

"What happened?"

"I'll let him tell you. Hang on."

She starts to move with the phone, heading for Billy's room. "Billy, your dad's on the phone."

I hear him grunt.

"I don't want to talk to him."

Um, thanks, Billy.

"Billy, your dad misses you, and he wants to talk to you."

"Fine. Whatever."

Billy's face appears on the screen, and a real scowl is etched there.

"Hey, bud. What's up?" I say softly.

"Nothin'."

"Mom said there was a problem at school today. You okay?"

His eyes flash up from the phone—at Tru, I'm guessing—his frown deepening. "Mom, you promised you wouldn't say anything."

"I didn't say anything, I swear," she says.

"B, your mom just told me that there was a problem at school, not what happened," I tell him, bringing his eyes to me. "You wanna talk to me about it?"

"No."

Um, okay.

"Anything else you wanna tell me about what happened today?"

He pauses for a minute, biting his lip. "Well…I did sign up for…guitar lessons at school."

"You did? That's awesome news!"

Finally, one of my kids is showing an interest in music. JJ is all about sports, and Belle is obsessed with princesses and apparently getting married.

A shy smile creeps across Billy's face.

"I can help show you some of the basics before your lessons start, if you want. Put you ahead of the class," I offer, wanting that smile to stay.

His eyes brighten, his smile getting wider. "Sure. That'd be cool, Dad."

"Okay, we'll do that tomorrow night when I get home. You and me, guitar lesson in my studio."

"Can't wait," he beams.

My heart elevates.

I made him happy, and that makes me beyond happy.

Look at me, total expert at fixing my kid's problem.

"Put your mom back on for me," I tell him. "And, B? I love you."

He pauses and smiles again. "Love you, too, Dad."

Seriously, there is nothing like hearing your kids tell you they love you. *Nothing.*

Tru's beautiful face appears back on the screen.

I can tell she's walking, so I ask quietly, "You out of earshot, babe?"

"Gimme one sec." I hear a door shut, and then she says, "Okay, go ahead."

"What did Billy do at school? I'm dying to know."

Her eyes fill with mirth, and she bites her lip. "Don't tell him I told you."

"I swear, I won't. Now, tell me."

"Well, he...*accidentally* killed the class goldfish," she whispers, humor in her voice.

I hold back a laugh. "And how did he manage that?"

"He fed it his lunch 'cause he thought it looked hungry."

I can't contain the laughter anymore, and it bursts from me. "How in the hell does a goldfish look hungry?"

Tru's eyes are shining, her lips trembling. "He said it was...skinny!"

Laughter erupts from her. By this point, I'm belly-laughing.

God, I fucking love my kids.

"Ah, fuck." I press my hand to my stomach. "I miss you guys."

"We miss you, too." She wipes the tears of humor from her face. "But you'll be home tomorrow, yeah?"

"Yeah. If all goes well, I'll be home tomorrow—hopefully, with good news that Storm's gonna come live with us." And that right there brings me back to the now.

Her face softens, all traces of playfulness gone. "It'll be fine, Jake. He'll just need time to adjust to the idea. But who wouldn't want to come live with us? We're awesome." She smiles.

"And this is why I love you," I tell her.

"The only reason?" She bites her lip again.

"Oh, no. I love you for a lot of other reasons, too—especially that amazing rack of yours. Now, take your top off, and show me your tits." I grin.

She laughs, deep and throaty. "Perv."

"Yeah, and you fucking love it."

"Wouldn't have married you if I didn't."

Then, she moves the phone back, so I can watch as she slowly starts to unbutton her shirt.

This is what I'm talking about.

My hand immediately goes to my dick over my jeans.

"Mama!" Belle yells out in the background.

For fucks sake!

I let out a groan of frustration, and Tru's eyes lift to the heavens as she chuckles.

"Tomorrow," she says. "And don't worry about Storm, babe. Things will work out exactly the way they're meant to." She presses her lips to the screen, sending me a kiss. "I love you," she whispers.

Then, she's gone, and I'm back to being alone in Jonny's bedroom, my hand on my dick.

I flop back on the bed. Lifting my arm, I look at my watch, seeing that it's five p.m.

I sit back up and speed-dial Tom's number. I'm hoping Denny's with him, so Tom can put me on speaker, and I can tell them at the same time how things went with Storm.

I just want to get this conversation over with, then get showered and changed, and head back to Storm's place, so I can try to actually spend some time with the kid.

THIRTEEN

We've just left Bob's house, and we are on our way to see Storm. The Rolling Stones' "Paint It Black" comes on the radio station.

Closing my eyes, I press my head back into the seat. I remember when Jonny used to play this rift on his guitar, and we'd jam to it. That was back in the earlier days before we started writing our own songs.

Opening my eyes, I turn my head to look at Bob. "I was thinking we could stop by the cemetery. I want to visit Jonny."

"When?" he asks.

"Now."

"Do we have time?" He glances at the clock on the dash.

"I won't be long. I just…want to see him."

His expression softens. "You don't have to explain it to me, son. I know." He pats my arm with his hand.

"Dave"—I lean forward in my seat—"change of plans. Woodlawn Cemetery first and then Queens."

Nodding, Dave indicates his understanding, changing lanes.

It doesn't take long to get to the cemetery. Dave parks the car, not far from where Jonny's buried.

I remove my seat belt. Reaching for the handle, I see Bob's not moving.

"Are you coming?" I ask him.

He shakes his head. "I was here a few days ago. You go and have some one-on-one time with him."

I give him a grateful smile.

Leaning forward, I say to Dave, "Stay here with Bob. I won't be long."

He looks back over his shoulder at me. His expression is one of concern, as it always is when I suggest solo trips. "I should come with you, just in case."

"I'll be fine. No one is around," I assure him, nodding at the almost empty cemetery.

Only one guy is here, a good distance away, tending to the surrounding gardens.

"Are you sure?"

"I'm sure." I pat his shoulder before getting out of the car.

I shut the door, and I get my ball cap from my jacket pocket and put it on. I pull the peak low, more out of habit than anything. I'm not exactly at risk of being mobbed here.

I walk the short distance down the tree-lined path, and then I cut across, heading for Jonny's grave. I slow my pace as I approach, my eyes landing on his mother's headstone.

Lyn is buried next to Jonny. Bob has the plot on the other side of Jonny for when he—

I don't want to think about that right now.

Coming to a stop at the foot of Jonny's grave, I crouch down, getting to my knees, and I press my hands to the grass. "Hey…so I met Storm earlier. God, I can't believe you have a son, Jon, and you never even got to meet him. It just feels…wrong. But I'm gonna take care of him. You don't have to worry. Your dad and I, Tom and Den, too— we've got his back. Anything he needs…"

Driving my hand through my hair, I blow out a breath.

"He's so much like you…it…" I turn my eyes away from his headstone, my fingers curling into the grass. "It fucking hurt to look at him. How crazy is that? It hurt to look at a kid. And I know, if you could right now, you'd tell me to shut my pussy ass up, get the fuck out of here, and go see your kid.

"I just…I wanted to see you before I saw him again. I was kinda hoping you'd show me a sign or some shit at how to best handle this with Storm. He's angry, Jon. He's thirteen, and his mom is dying. He just found out about you being his dad, and he's pissed.

"Honestly, I'm pissed for him. I'm…fucking mad at you for dying. I've always been mad at you for that—now, even more so. Why the fuck did you get in your car that night." I grit my teeth, shaking my head. "I just wish…I wish you'd known about him, Jon. Maybe it would have changed things. Made you stop using drugs. Maybe you would never have gotten in your car that night—no, not maybe. You wouldn't have. I have to believe that. I have to believe that, if you'd known about Storm, then you would have sorted your shit out and got clean for him."

Shaking my head, I let out a humorless chuckle.

"Hindsight—it's a motherfucker, ain't it?"

I stare ahead at nothing for a moment. Then, I push up to my feet and put my hands in my pockets. I look at Jonny's name etched deep into the headstone.

"I miss you, man."

Then, I turn on my heel and head back to the car.

FOURTEEN

When we pull up in front of the bakery, it's closed, but the lights are on.

Bob and I exit the car. Dave isn't staying this time. He's going to have dinner with an old friend and come back to pick us up in a few hours.

I knock on the glass door. A few seconds later, Marie appears. She unlocks the door, letting us in. She isn't smiling at me, but she isn't scowling either, so I take that as a good thing.

I hear Dave's car pulling away as Marie closes the door behind us.

"Go on up," she tells us.

I lead the way, and Bob follows me through the back and up the stairs. When I reach the landing, I knock on the apartment door.

I hear voices behind the door. Then, it opens, and Storm is standing on the other side.

Only a few hours ago, I saw him, but the sight of him is still a sucker-punch to the heart. I wonder if seeing him will ever stop hurting.

"Hey," he says in a low tone, his eyes sweeping the floor. "Come in."

He stands aside, so Bob and I walk in.

There's an awkward moment where we're all standing in the hallway with no clue about what to say.

"Mom's already at the table," he says.

He starts walking, so we follow him. He turns into a kitchen with a small table in the center. Tiffany is sitting at it. She doesn't look well—not that she looked well earlier, but she seems a little worse now.

I start to wonder if we should be here. She looks like she needs rest.

"Hey," I say to her. "Are you okay?"

"Fine." She gives me a bright smile, but I can tell it's forced. "Sit, please." She gestures to the empty chairs.

Storm sits opposite Tiffany, so Bob and I take the two seats opposite each other. Lasagna and salad are already on the table.

"Looks great." I gesture to the food.

"I can't take credit. Marie made it for us. I don't get to cook much nowadays." Her smile is forced again.

"I don't cook ever." I laugh.

"Yeah, you probably have a maid to do all that for you," Storm mutters.

Okay...

I see a look transpire between Tiffany and Storm.

So, I chuckle and say, "Well, I wouldn't call my wife a maid. I wouldn't dare. She'd have my ass if I did."

Even though Tru would look amazing in a maid's uniform. Maybe I should buy her one—for bedroom purposes only, of course.

"You don't have house staff?" Storm frowns at me.

"We do have a cleaner who comes in a once a week to help out, but we have three kids, and my wife works. That's it though."

He looks at me like he doesn't believe me.

"I do have staff…people who work for me at the label."

My eyes flicker to Bob, realizing what I'm talking about—the label that Jonny and I set up together. Maybe I shouldn't have brought it up.

"You know, when Jake and Jonny created TMS Records, they were the youngest people ever to own and run their own label," Bob tells Storm.

My eyes come back to Bob, and he gives me a smile.

Picking up the bottle of water from the table, I pour some out before offering it to everyone else.

"So, who do you have signed to your label then?" Storm asks with a begrudging tone, but he's talking to me. So, I run with it.

"We have The Devil's Own, and of course, Vintage—"

"I love their music," Tiffany says.

"Oh, and we've just signed Lennox," I add.

"Lennox?" Storm's eyes show immediate interest.

"Yeah. You like them?"

"*Like* is putting it mildly." Tiffany laughs softly.

"Yeah, well, they're awesome," Storm says defensively, in only that way a teenager can.

"I can arrange for you to meet them sometime, if you'd like," I tell him.

"Really?" His face is all lit up.

I know that I'm making some ground with him. Even if only a small amount, it's a move in the right direction.

We spend the rest of dinner talking about bands we like. Storm tells us about songs he can play on his guitar. I ask him to get his guitar and play some for us, but he declines. He does that embarrassed look that my kids do when they don't want to do something, so I don't push it with Storm. There will be plenty of time to hear his abilities even though I am dying to see if he plays like Jonny did.

"That lasagna was amazing." Bob presses his hand to his stomach. "Thank Marie for us."

"She'll be pleased to hear that you enjoyed it," Tiffany says.

"Well, let us clean up since you fed us." Bob stands, picking up his plate.

"No, it's fine." Tiffany waves him down.

But I know that there's no way she can stand at the sink, washing dishes, with how sick she is.

"It's no trouble. And my wife would have my ass if she knew I hadn't offered to clean up." I stand, collecting the rest of the plates. I take them over to the sink.

"Bob, why don't you and Tiffany go sit in the living room, and Storm and I will do the dishes?"

Storm's eyes flash to mine. For a moment, he looks like he's going to argue, and then he seems to relent.

"Sure. You go rest, Mom." He stands. Going over to the sink, he starts to fill it with water, adding dish washing liquid.

"I'll wash," I tell him, rolling up my sleeves. I have no clue where the dishes need to go, so it'll be easier this way.

Storm brings the rest of the dishes over, and I start washing.

After I place the washed plate on the dish drainer, he picks it up and starts to dry it with a dish towel.

"Not very rock and roll," he says. "Never thought I'd see the day when Jake Wethers was standing in my kitchen, washing the dishes. I almost feel like I should take a picture." He chuckles.

"Yeah, don't." I laugh. "Tom and Den would never let me live it down."

He chuckles again, and then silence descends between us as we wash the dishes.

"What was he like?" His softly spoken words blindside me. There's an ache to them, and it's like a blade piercing my chest.

I turn my eyes to him, to find him already watching me.

"Jonny?" I'm careful not to call Jonny his dad. I don't want to pour fuel on Storm's kindling flame.

"Yeah," he utters, his eyes sweeping the floor.

I stare down into the soapy water my hands are in. "He was wild, impulsive, and stubborn. But he was loyal, talented and smart as hell." A smile plays on my lips. "He could play a guitar like you'd never seen before. And…he was my best friend." A lump chokes my throat. I turn, pressing my back against the counter. "You look exactly like he did at your age."

"You knew him when he was young?"

"Yeah." I give him a sad smile.

Storm turns away. Walking over to a cupboard, he puts a plate away and closes the cupboard door. Still facing away, he says, "I read some stuff on the Internet…about Jonny. It said…well, it said that…he killed himself."

My body tenses up.

Storm turns to face me, leaning back against the counter.

I look him in the eyes. "Jonny didn't kill himself." I try to keep my voice even. "He had too much to live for. He just…he made a really bad decision that night when he climbed into his car. It was an accident. A *tragic* accident."

I want to tell Storm that Jonny would never have even been in that situation if he'd known about Storm, but it'd sound like I was blaming Tiffany for the choices she'd made, and I don't want to do that.

Shifting on his feet, he glances down at them. "Look…I know there was a chance that you could have been my dad." His eyes flick back up to mine.

I can't hide the surprise on my face.

"I overheard Mom talking to Marie one day."

"Oh."

"I know Mom was wild back in the day."

I don't know what to say. What does he want me to say?

Fuck. I'm not prepared for this.

He wraps his arms around his stomach. "I bet you were relieved when you found out that I wasn't your kid," he utters. "I know you have this perfect family. You wouldn't want someone like me coming along and screwing it up."

I blow out a breath, gripping the edge of the counter with my hands. "Look, Storm, I can't deny that if you'd been mine, it would have made things difficult for me for a while. But if you'd been my blood, there wouldn't have been a second when I wouldn't have wanted you."

I want to make him feel better. I know he's hurting, and I want to take that away.

And it's not a lie. If he had been my son, no matter how much it would have hurt Tru, hurt us all, I would never have turned him away.

"And I know, without a doubt, that Jonny would have been the same, if he were here," I say, impassioned.

"But he's not here."

"No, he's not. But I am, and so is Bob. And we want…" Taking a pause, I pull in a breath, making sure I word this just right. "We want to be your family, too."

His expression shuts down, and he turns his face away from me, tossing the dish towel on the counter. "You all right to finish up here? I have homework to do," he says without looking at me.

"Yeah," I say, holding the disappointment from my voice. "I'm good. You go."

THE STORM

Then, Storm walks out of the kitchen without another word, leaving me standing there, knowing I still have a hell of a ways to go with this kid.

FIFTEEN

I finish up the dishes and head into the living room. Tiffany and Bob are sitting on the sofa, and she's showing him baby pictures of Storm.

"Everything okay?" Bob asks, a touch of concern in his voice.

Maybe the expression on my face has him worried. Or maybe it's because Storm isn't with me.

"Yeah, everything's fine. Storm's gone to do his homework."

"Voluntarily?" Tiffany smiles. "That's a first."

"He asked about Jonny."

"Oh," she says. "He hasn't...he hasn't asked me a thing about him. What did...what did he want to know?"

"What Jonny was like. And..." I glance at the doorway and then lower my voice as I say, "He knows there was a chance he could have been mine."

"Oh." Her eyes widen.

"He said he overheard you talking to Marie."

"Shit," she says. "Should I go talk to him?"

I shake my head. "He didn't seem overly upset about it."

She glances at the door and then says, "Still, I'll talk to him about it. Tomorrow though. Probably not best to do it today."

"I also told him that we want to be his family." My eyes go to Bob.

He lifts his brows. "And what was his response?"

"He said nothing. That was when he went to do his homework." I say quietly, "Maybe I pushed it a little too far too soon?"

Bob lifts his lips at the corners. "You've never been one for patience, Jake."

Can't argue with that.

I can feel Tiffany's eyes on me. When I look at her, I see concern there.

"Look, I don't know what exactly you want from us. If it's money to secure Storm's future, then that's a given. Anything he needs, he can have."

"Jonny's money," Bob says. "I'm going to put it into a trust for Storm."

Bob didn't discuss that with me, but I'm not surprised.

"He doesn't need all that money," she tells him.

"I'm an old man. I'm the one who doesn't need that money," Bob counters.

"Look"—she presses her hands to her lap—"we just need to lay this out there. I know talking about death makes people uncomfortable, but it's a fact of life. We're all going to die someday. Unfortunately, my day is coming sooner than I wanted. I wanted to see Storm grow and have his own children, but that's not going to happen."

Her eyes are glazing with sadness, and I feel a tug in my gut.

Bob reaches over and takes ahold of her hand. She gratefully smiles at him.

"I want Storm to be financially secure, of course I do. And I knew I was taking a risk in finding out if he was Jonny's, with him no longer being alive, and I knew either way, no matter the outcome, if he was Jake or Jonny's, that would give Storm financial security. But money aside…more than anything, I want him to have a family. Marie has offered to take him, and that would be good because he knows her…but—" She bites her lip. "I know he looks like Jonny…but a big part of me hoped…I'm sorry—" Her tear-filled eyes go to Bob. "But I wanted Storm to be Jake's son so that he wouldn't be alone when I die."

Fuck.

That punches a crater-sized hole in my chest.

"I don't want him to be alone when I'm gone. I don't want him to be an orphan. I want him to have a family."

"He has a family," Bob firmly tells her.

"He has us," I say. "And Tom and Denny. All of us—we're his family." I push my hand through my hair, and I decide to just go for broke. Like Bob said, patience really isn't my thing. "Look…" I choose not to look at Bob when I say this, instead just focusing on Tiffany. "Bob and I have spoken, and we both have agreed. If you do, too, then…we want Storm and you to come to live in LA. Bob is moving in with my family and me, and I'll set you up with whatever you need. You can live out your time there, and it will give Storm time to get to know us, help him settle. Then, when the time comes"—*when you're gone*—"Storm will move in with us—my family and me."

Her eyes widen, tears glazing them. "How does your wife feel about this?"

"Trust me, if I didn't have her backing, I wouldn't have said these things right now."

"You want to take Storm on as your own, have him live with you? Why?"

I'm surprised she even has to ask. "He's Jonny's flesh and blood. That makes him mine—ours." I flicker a glance at Bob, who gives me a subtle nod of encouragement. "Jonny would have done the same for me, if I weren't here. He would have taken care of my kid. I want to take care of his."

Then, she bursts into tears, and I honestly don't know what to do.

I flick a panicked glance at Bob.

"Here, don't cry." He pulls a handkerchief from his pocket and hands it to her.

She dries her face. "I'm sorry." She sniffles. "I just...thank you." She meets my eyes and then Bob's. "I can't tell you what a relief it is to know that you want to do this for Storm."

"And you, too." Bob pats her hand.

"But...how will this work? Of course I want to take you up on this offer—for Storm—but Marie...she's my friend. She's been my family for so long. I don't want to leave her."

"Don't worry," I tell her. "We'll figure things out with Marie."

"And Storm...moving him from everything he knows is going to be hard on him."

"Things are already hard on him." At the wince on her face, I say, "I don't mean to sound harsh, but we need to be realistic here, and being realistic means, there will be changes, changes that will affect him. But if we implement those changes *now*"—I put the emphasis on *now* because I really don't want to say, *While you are still alive to help him*—"it will help to make this transition as easy as it can possibly be for Storm."

"That's all I care about," Tiffany says, looking me in the eyes, "that Storm is okay."

I wrap my arms around my chest. "He will be okay. I don't have all the fine details worked out. And I don't know exactly how this will all work, but it will work, Tiffany. Storm will be okay," I promise.

SIXTEEN

Tiffany said she would call after she'd spoken with Storm about moving to LA. I didn't hear from her last night after we'd left her apartment. I assume, if she had talked to him then, it might have been too late to call me.

Not that I slept great. After calling Tru, followed by a quick call to Stuart, I spent the night tossing and turning.

A lot was riding on this for me. I didn't want to let Jonny down by failing Storm in any way.

And I like to be in control of everything. I haven't felt a lack of control like this since Tru's accident, and it's not a feeling I like to be reminded of.

My cell starts to ring just as I'm making coffee.

It's early. Bob and Dave aren't up yet. I think Bob needs the sleep. This last week must have been exhausting for him.

Picking up my cell from the counter, I see Tiffany is calling.

"Hi," I answer.

"Morning," she says. "I hope I'm not calling too early?"

"I've been up. So…how did it go?"

"Not as bad as I had expected."

Relief seeps from me.

"I mean, he kicked up a little fuss to start with, but then he got excited about the idea of living in LA. And I might have sold him on it with…well, I said that he could probably meet your band, Lennox—the one he loves— more than once, if he were living in LA."

I let out a small laugh. "Bribery—it always works with my kids. I'm beyond glad that he's on board. I spoke to Tru last night, and we're going to sort out a place for you guys to live and schooling for Storm. You don't need to worry about anything."

"Thank you."

"What about Marie?" I ask. "Have you talked to her yet?"

"Yeah. She…she wants to come with us. She wants to be there for me when…you know."

"Yeah, I know. I can arrange for someone to run her bakery while she's away, if that would work for her."

"She mentioned bringing someone in. Maybe talk to her about it?"

"I'll have Stuart call her. He'll sort it out."

"Stuart, your old PA? He's still with you?"

"I'm not easy to leave." I laugh. "He couldn't live without me."

"Somehow, I think that's the other way around."

"Totally," I concede, chuckling. "And Stuart will be in touch to arrange getting your stuff packed up and moved there."

There's a pause.

Then, she says, "Thank you...for all of this. I can't begin to tell you how much of a weight has been lifted off my shoulders, knowing that Storm's going to be...well, that he'll have you taking care of him when I'm gone."

"Whatever he needs. And you, too...anything you need."

"Thank you. Again. And I guess I'll see you in LA soon."

"You will."

I watch as the car pulls up the drive.

I feel Tru's hand tightening around mine. "Nervous?" I ask, glancing down at her.

"What if Storm doesn't like me?"

"Impossible." I brush my fingers over the soft skin on her cheek.

Her lips lift a little at the corners.

Dave picked Tiffany, Storm, and Marie up from the airport and brought them straight here.

This was Tiffany's idea. She thought it'd be best for Storm to come straight to the place that would eventually, hopefully, be his home and meet us before going to their new place.

I wasn't sure she would be up to it after the flight, but she assured me she would be fine.

They get out of the car, Marie helping Tiffany, and my eyes are on Storm, watching his reaction.

Tru is the first to approach them.

"Hey, Storm. I'm Tru." She smiles that big beautiful smile of hers. Then, she clasps ahold of his upper arms and kisses him on the cheek.

Right then, in that moment, I see that she has him. His eyes light up with surprise and then soften on her.

"Hi." He smiles back at her wide and warm.

He's never smiled at me like that.

For a split-second, I actually feel jealous of my wife.

That's all she has to do, just smile, and she has the kid like putty in her hands. Then again, that's all she did to me to get me all those years ago.

Tiffany comes to stand by her son, and I stay back a little as I watch Tru move from Storm to Tiffany.

"Tiffany, I'm Tru. It's really nice to finally meet you." She greets Tiffany in the same way, kissing her cheek.

"It's great to meet you," Tiffany says. I hear a touch of nerves in her voice. "This is my best friend, Marie." Tiffany gestures to Marie, who is standing beside her.

"Nice to meet you." Marie sticks her hand out to Tru.

Tru glances down at her hand and then shakes it.

Guess Marie isn't down with my wife's greeting style.

"Dada!" Belle's squealing voice comes from behind me, and then her arms are wrapping around my leg. "Is Stwowm here? Is this them?"

"I tried to keep her inside, but she broke free." Stuart laughs.

I glance over my shoulder and see Stuart walking toward us, with Bob, and then, JJ and Billy are coming out, too.

Bob moved into Stuart's old place on the grounds. He wouldn't move into the house. He said we didn't need an old man cramping our style. But he's still in our house more than his own, and the kids love having him here.

So do I.

I realize now that I should have talked him into moving here after Lyn had passed. I failed then. I won't make that mistake again.

And I intend on not making any mistakes with Storm, now that I have him here.

I pick up Belle and gesture for JJ and Billy to come over.

"Storm, Tiffany, and Marie." I point to each of them, so my kids know who they are. "These are my kids—JJ"—I pat his head beside me—"Billy"—I touch his shoulder—"and Belle, the monkey in my arms."

"Not monkey." Belle scowls at me and then wriggles out of my arms to be put down.

I put her on her feet, and she walks over to Storm. She stares at him, and he watches her.

With fascination, I keep my eyes on Belle's curious face.

When she stops before him, he crouches down to eye-level with her.

"Hey," he says softly.

"You like pwincesses?" she asks him.

"Answer carefully," Tru says with a touch of humor in her voice. "Your entire existence might depend on this."

Storm smiles up at Tru and then looks back to Belle, still smiling. "I think princesses are the best things ever."

Belle beams at him. "Wanna play pwincesses with me?"

"'Course he doesn't wanna play princesses with you." Billy goes over to them. "He's a boy. Boys don't like princesses."

"They do, too." Belle scowls at Billy.

"I got a guitar," Billy tells Storm. "My dad's helping me learn how to play."

"I play guitar," Storm says.

"Cool."

"My dad has a studio in the house," JJ pipes up from beside me. "You wanna come see?"

Storm glances over at him and smiles. "Sure."

He stands, and then Belle reaches up and grabs his hand. I see the surprise on his face as he stares down at her.

Then, he glances over at Tiffany.

I look at her, too. I see the emotion in her eyes, and then she gives him a gentle nod, telling him to go on ahead.

I watch as Belle leads Storm into my house, Billy and JJ with them. All three of them start firing off questions at Storm.

"Kids make life seem so easy," Bob says from behind me.

"Yeah, they do," I say, turning to him.

"I made coffee," Stuart tells me.

That's his way of saying I should invite my guests in.

I turn back to Tru, who is quietly chatting with Tiffany and Marie.

"Stuart made coffee," I tell them.

I let everyone pass me, heading into the house. I hang back, catching Tru's hand, as she passes. I slide my arm around her waist.

"You okay?" I ask her. "I know that couldn't have been easy for you."

"I'm fine." She turns her body into mine, wrapping her arms around me. "How are you?"

"Okay," I say. And I really am. I will always be okay, so long as I have her.

I lean down and brush my lips over hers. "Thank you."

"For?" she whispers against my mouth.

"For just being you. I love you."

"I love you, too. Now, let's get in there and save poor Storm before Belle has him married off to one of her princess dolls." Tru laughs.

And it's in this moment, I just know that everything is going to be okay.

Everything will work out as it should.

Two Months Later

Storm and I are sitting on some chairs in the corridor, out by Tiffany's room. The doctor is in with her.

Tiffany isn't doing well at all. She's been deteriorating rapidly these past few weeks. I don't think she has much longer left.

I arranged for Tiffany to see the best doctors LA had to offer, and they took over her treatment.

But her cancer is too advanced. There's nothing anyone can do for her, except to make her as comfortable as possible.

A week ago, Tiffany had to be moved into the hospital permanently, as she now needs round-the-clock care, and her doctor advised this was the best place for her.

So, Storm has been living with Marie at their house.

I want him to move in with us now, but I don't want to push it even though we've been getting closer recently.

Bob, Tom, Denny, and I have been spending a lot of time with Storm. We want him to feel like he's a part of the family. And I think we're getting there.

My kids love Storm. From that first moment they met him, it was like they'd always known him.

He's been building a real bond with them. It's amazing to see.

Tru has been incredible. She's been spending time with Tiffany, getting to know her better. I know that couldn't have been easy for her. She did it for me but more for Storm.

He loves her. I can see it in the way he looks at her. And Tru loves him right back.

They've developed a great friendship. More so recently, as Tiffany has been deteriorating, he's been turning to Tru when he wants to talk.

I'm so fucking lucky to have Tru.

When I think about what's happening to Tiffany and how I came so close to losing Tru after her accident, it makes me hold her for that much longer, makes me tell her how much I love her so many more times.

I know how fortunate I am to have her here with me. And I will never take that for granted for one second.

"How you doing?" I ask Storm, who's staring intently at his cell, playing on some game.

He's been quieter lately, which isn't surprising. He's had a lot of changes in his life.

A new city. A new school.

His mother's illness getting worse.

I can't even imagine how hard it is for him at the moment.

Storm doesn't get a chance to answer as a shadow falls over us, and I look up to see Tiffany's doctor, Dr. Munson, standing before us.

"Jake, can I have a word?"

"Sure." Getting up, I tell Storm, "I'll only be a minute."

I follow Dr. Munson a little farther down the corridor until we're a ways from Storm.

"There's no easy way to say this…" He folds his arms over his chest. "The new drugs we put Tiffany on aren't helping her anymore."

I blow out a breath. "How long?"

"A week—at the most."

"Hell." I close my eyes on a blink as I blow out a breath, my mind immediately going to that kid sitting down the hall.

Even though we knew this was coming, it doesn't make it any easier to hear.

"Tiffany has asked to see you—*alone*," he emphasizes, his eyes moving to look at Storm.

I get the message loud and clear. *Don't tell Storm anything.*

"Okay." I leave Dr. Munson, and I walk back over to Storm.

His eyes lift from his phone to me as I approach.

"I'm just gonna go in and see your mom, alone, for a minute. Then, I'll come get you. Okay?"

"Yeah. Whatever." His eyes go back to his phone.

I know he's trying to act like he doesn't care, doesn't want to know why his mother wants to see me alone, but I know he does.

I stare at him for a moment, feeling an ache so deep in my chest that it would take a miracle to get it out.

Leaving Storm, I walk to Tiffany's room and push open the door, letting myself in.

Her head is turned, and she's staring out the window.

She looks so small in that big bed.

She moves her eyes over to me when she hears me enter.

"Hey." She smiles. "Dr. Munson talk to you?"

"Yeah, he did," I say gently as I sit down on the chair by her bed.

"You didn't tell Storm?"

"No." I shake my head.

"Thank you. I want to be the one to tell him…you know?" She blows out a breath. "But I wanted to talk to you first because…well, I want to thank you for everything you've done for us—bringing us here, accepting Storm into your family."

"You don't need to thank me."

"I do. You are a good person, Jake Wethers, and don't let anyone ever tell you any different. God, back in those early days, you used to terrify me." She laughs softly. "All that natural confidence and arrogance is intimidating. Yet I still wanted to be close to you. Same with Jonny. Moth-to-flame syndrome with you two. Most girls had it around you both."

I let out a chuckle. "Not most. All."

"And there it is." She laughs again. "I'm glad you're happy. You picked real well with Tru. She's amazing."

"She picked me, not the other way around. And trust me, I'm the lucky one."

"You're both lucky." She smiles again, but then she starts to cough.

Bringing a tissue to her mouth, she coughs into it. I see small speckles of blood on it.

"You need me to get the doctor?"

"No. Just some water."

I hand her the cup, and when she's finished, I take it from her.

"Would you grab that envelope for me, over on the table?" She points to a brown envelope by the flowers on the table in the corner of her room.

Getting up, I go over and get it. Sitting down, I hand it to her, but she pushes it back into my hand.

"These are for you, if you want them. I talked to Bob, and he agrees with me. You and Tru have everything to offer Storm. Bob's old, and of course, he'll be in Storm's life, but I want Storm to have a family, a *real* family, the one thing I never gave him."

"You gave him a family," I counter.

She gently shakes her head. "I gave him the best I could, but I never gave him his dad. That was the biggest mistake of my life. If I could change it, I would. But if you want to...I want you and Tru to adopt him."

I pull the papers from the envelope, seeing the wording at the top.

"Bob sorted it out with his lawyer for me. We've taken all the necessary steps, and I have signed all the papers. They just need your and Tru's signatures now, and then it'll be legal and binding."

"Does Storm know about this?"

"He will when I talk to him. I wanted to talk to you first and make sure you wanted him—"

"I want him," I say without hesitation.

"And what about Tru?" she asks. "Will she be okay with this?"

"Tru loves Storm. You don't need to worry. Adopting Storm is something Tru and I have already discussed."

I see the relief flicker through Tiffany's eyes.

"So, we're agreed then."

Putting the papers back into the envelope, I hold them to my chest. "Yeah, we're agreed."

She exhales. "Good. Now, would you mind getting Storm for me, so I can speak to him?"

"Sure." Getting up, I cross the room.

When I reach the door with my hand on the handle, I turn back to her. "Thank you," I tell her sincerely, "for giving me back..." My words choke in my throat, and I blink the tears away.

"I know," she says, bringing my eyes back to her. "I just...I wish I hadn't been that scared kid all those years ago. I wish...Jonny had known him."

Yeah, me, too.

But wishes are no good now.

Now, we make the best of what we have. And I have Jonny's son to take care of.

Giving Tiffany a small nod, I press down on the handle and leave the room, my fingers curled around the envelope.

One Week Later

Tiffany passed away two days after she'd given me the adoption papers. Storm, Marie, and Bob were with her when she passed.

This week has been beyond difficult for Storm. But Tru and I have made sure that he knows he has us, that we aren't going anywhere.

The adoption is in process. I'm having my lawyer work hard to push it through quickly.

Storm came to stay with us the night Tiffany died, and then he asked if he could stay the next night.

He's been here ever since. I think it might have been too difficult for him to go back to the place where they lived together during these last couple of months. And I think my kids help take his mind off of it, keeping him busy. He and Billy have been spending time in my home studio. He's been helping Billy with learning how to play the guitar.

Marie is still staying in the house I rented for them. She hasn't told me her plans yet, but I know, at some point, she will go back to Queens, back to her bakery. At the moment, her presence is a familiarity for Storm, a needed tie to his old life, so I'm hoping she'll hang around a little while longer.

We had the funeral service this morning. It was small and intimate.

As Tiffany hadn't had contact with her parents since Storm was born, we'd asked Storm if he wanted to let them know about her death and invite them to the funeral, but he'd said no.

So, it was just me, Tru, Storm, and Marie at the funeral. Tom, Lyla, Denny, Simone, Stuart, and Josh came, too.

We didn't take the kids to Tiffany's funeral. They stayed home with Tru's mom and dad.

And that's where we are now. Everyone came back to our house for some food, not that many of us feel like eating though.

I'm in the kitchen, pouring myself out a finger of whiskey, when I hear movement behind me.

Glancing over my shoulder, I see Marie. She has a pinched expression on her face. Marie and I aren't what I would call friends. I've felt an animosity from her since the day we met, but she's important to Storm, so I make nice with her.

"Is Storm okay?" I ask her, putting the bottle down.

"He's fine—well, as fine as he can be. He's with the other kids in the game room."

Picking up my glass, I turn to face her. "You want one?" I gesture to my whiskey.

"No." She shakes her head. "I was…look, can we talk?"

"Sure. Go ahead." I take a sip of my drink.

She glances around the kitchen, as though she expects someone to walk in at any moment.

"What I want to talk about…is…delicate. Is there somewhere private we could talk?"

"Outside?" I nod in the direction of the garden.

"Sure."

Leading the way, I head out back with Marie following me.

I take a seat at the outdoor table where we eat a lot of our meals, and I place my glass on the table.

Marie takes the seat across from me. She briefly looks at me and then looks away, blowing out a breath.

The silence is bugging me. "So, what did you want to talk to me about?"

"I don't really know how to start," she says.

The nerves and uncertainty in her voice make the nape of my neck prickle. She looks like she's having an internal battle with herself.

I sit up a little straighter, picking up my whiskey.

The movement catches her attention.

"I need to tell you something, something I should have told Tiffany, but I was afraid to tell her. I didn't, and I've kept it in for all these years. Then, she got sick."

Her eyes meet with mine, and I see a flash of tears and remorse in them.

"I didn't want her to die hating me."

"Why would she have hated you?" My mouth is dry, so I take another sip of whiskey, my hand tightening around the glass.

"I just…I can't keep it in anymore. It's been eating me up inside. If anyone deserves the truth, aside from Tiffany and Storm, it's you."

I swallow down. "What truth?"

"The night…that Jonny died." She blows out a shallow breath through her teeth. "It was my fault…that he died."

I slam my glass down on the table, making her jump.

"What do you mean, it was your fault?" My voice sounds harsh because I'm barely holding on to my restraint.

"The night he died, I spoke to him on the phone."

"Why? How? Did you know him?"

She shakes her head. "I didn't know him. I have a friend, and he got me Jonny's number. Tiffany…she had never told me who Storm's father was.

"One night, when Storm was five, she went out with this guy she was dating. I was watching Storm for her. He was sleeping, and I was in my bedroom reading when she got in. I was surprised she was home, as it was early. I heard her in the living room, music playing, so I went to see how her date was. She was upset, crying. They'd broken up. She'd been drinking. She was listening to *your* music. Then, she just started talking. She told me all about her life before she came to Queens—how she was a groupie, how she spent a lot of time with The Mighty Storm, how you guys all lived your lives with the drugs, endless parties, and crazy sex. She said about her getting pregnant with Storm, her family kicking her out…and who Storm's father was."

She meets my eyes.

"Tiffany told me she'd been sleeping with both you and Jonny when she got pregnant. In the beginning, she wasn't sure who his father was, but the older Storm got, she knew, without a doubt, that Jonny was his father. Storm looked too much like Jonny not to be his son. I tried to encourage her to get in contact with Jonny and tell him.

"I grew up without knowing my father, Jake. My mother kept his identity from me. And I know how hard it is, not knowing where you came from, always feeling like you're missing a part of yourself. I didn't want that for Storm. But Tiffany wouldn't have it. She didn't want Storm to be a part of the lifestyle you all led. We disagreed about it. But she told me it was none of my business. Then, she left, heading to bed.

"I didn't agree, and I knew she was wrong. So...I called up my friend, who—well, it doesn't matter who he was or how he got Jonny's number. But he did.

"An hour later, I called Jonny's cell. It was really late in Queens, around one a.m., but I knew Jonny lived in LA, and I figured he wasn't the type of guy to go to bed early. I told him about Storm. He didn't believe me at first. Then, he remembered Tiffany. He wanted to see a picture of Storm, so I texted him one. And after that, he...I think he realized that Storm was his. He demanded that I give him Tiffany's address, said that he was coming to Queens, catching a flight out, and I couldn't tell her, so I didn't. I hung up with him, and I went to bed.

"When I woke up the next morning, Storm was in the kitchen, eating breakfast, and Tiffany was sitting in the living room, staring at the TV, crying. It was covered with pictures of Jonny's crash."

She swipes a tear from the corner of her eye.

"I knew it was my fault. He'd left his house that night and gotten in his car because of the phone call I'd made to him."

I can't breathe. I push up from my chair and stalk away, over to the outside bar. I refill my glass up to the top and down half of it. My hand is shaking.

When I turn around, Marie is standing by the table.

"He died because of me. But he died knowing he had a son."

My eyes start to sting.

He knew.

He knew he had a son, and he was going to get Storm, to claim him.

A tear runs from the corner of my eye. I roughly brush it away.

The back door opens, and Tru steps out.

I can't do anything but stare at her.

"Is everything okay out here?" Tru asks, glancing between Marie and me.

"I'm heading back to Queens today," Marie says to me. "I understand that you'll tell Storm. Just…tell him, I'm sorry."

Then, she turns and brushes past Tru, walking back into my house.

I'm rooted to the ground.

"Babe?" Tru is advancing toward me. "What happened?"

Fumbling to put the glass down on the bar top, I lean against it as she stands before me, reaching for my hand.

"He knew. Jonny knew about Storm." Another tear breaks free. "Right before he died…that's why…that's why he was out in his car. He was driving to the airport to catch a flight. He was going to see his son." I press the heel of my hand against the ache in my chest. "How the hell am I supposed to tell Storm this? I don't…" I roughly shake my head.

"Talk me through this, Jake. Tell me everything." She guides me over to the seats. "We'll figure this out together. It's going to be okay."

"Figure out what?" Tom says, coming through the open back door, pulling my eyes to him.

Denny is right behind him.

"You alone?" I ask them.

"Yeah." Denny gives me a puzzled look.

"Good. You're gonna want to sit down. I've got something to tell you."

BONUS CHAPTER

Eight Years Ago

Jonny

My fingers strum over the strings of the guitar lying across my lap as I stare out at the glittering city below me from my castle in the sky.

For once, I'm alone.

I'm never alone. If I'm not with the guys, there's always some chick ready to warm my bed.

But tonight, I wanted to be alone.

Recently, I've felt like something's missing. There's this emptiness inside me, and it's growing, no matter how much I try to fill it with drugs and alcohol and empty one-night stands.

Picking up the bottle of whiskey from the table beside me, I lift it to my lips, taking a long drink.

My cell starts to ring on the table, pulling my eyes to it.

Unknown number.

I'm just about to ignore it when I realize the area code is in New York.

My first thought is that it must be my folks.

I pick up my cell, answering, "Yeah?"

There's a brief silence on the line.

I consider hanging up when a soft female voice says, "Is this Jonny Creed?"

"Who is this?"

"My name is Marie. I'm a friend of—"

"Look, I'm sure you're hot and that you love my music, but not right now, honey, okay?"

"No, wait. That's not why I'm calling. Look, there's no easy way to say this, but...you have a son."

I bark out a laugh.

Then, it dawns on me. *Fucking Tom.*

"Sure I do, honey. You can put Tom on the phone now. Tom, you bastard, I know it's you."

The fucker is always pranking me. I didn't know he was in New York though.

"I'm not with anyone called Tom. And no one put me up to this, Jonny. This isn't a joke. You have a son. He's five years old. His mother's name is Tiffany Slater. She used to be a groupie, hung around with you and the band about six years ago. You and she used to...you know...be *together.*"

Tiffany Slater…

I know that name.

Six years ago…

I search through the catalog of women in my mind. I've slept with a lot of women, but six years ago were the early days. The women were a plenty, even back then, but we stuck around with a group of girls—

Then, it hits me.

Tiffany. Blonde hair. Pretty as hell. Legs that went on forever.

"I remember her. She just stopped coming around all of a sudden."

"She stopped coming around because she was pregnant. She told me she wasn't sure at the time if he was your child or Jake's. But she knows now, and it's blatantly obvious that he's yours. He looks exactly like you."

"If she was fucking me and Jake, she could have been fucking a hundred other guys. No reason to believe this kid is mine."

"She wasn't. It was only you and Jake. And she had genuine real feelings for you, Jonny. I'm telling you. Storm is your son."

That causes me pause. "His name is Storm?"

"Yes. I'm guessing she named him after your band." I hear her exhale down the phone. "I'm not making this up. I have no reason to make this up. There's no win in this for me."

"So, why are you telling me now?"

"I've known Tiffany for a long time, and in all that time she never told me who Storm's father is. Then, tonight…she was upset. She'd been drinking. She told me the truth."

"And the first thing you do is call me? Some friend you are."

"I am being her friend," she says defensively. "She kept Storm from you because of the life you lead. But she struggles every day. She works her ass off to put food on the table for that boy. And I believe that every child should know both of their parents."

I look down and realize my hand is shaking. I clench it into a fist. "You honestly believe this kid is mine?" I know she does, I can hear it in her voice.

"Yes. I honestly do."

I can barely believe I'm having this conversation, but something is pulling on the fringes of my subconscious.

There's always been something missing. Maybe this is it.

Taking a deep breath, I blow it out. "Do you have a picture of him?" I ask quietly.

"I have one on my cell. It was taken the other day."

"Send it to me now. I want to see him."

"I'll have to disconnect the call to send it."

"I don't care. Just send me the fucking picture."

I hang up the call and wait.

It seems to take forever before my cell beeps with a text.

I take a fortifying breath.

This is stupid. I'm being stupid. This kid isn't mine. She's just some psycho chick making crank calls.

But...what if she's not?

Decision made, I open the text, click on the picture, and stare at my screen, waiting for it to load.

Then, it does.

Holy fuck.

I can't breathe. Staring back at me is a blue-eyed little boy with dirty-blond hair and a smile that could bring the sun down, and he looks exactly like me.

But how can I be sure? He might just be a kid who looks like me.

Looks a lot like me.

His eyes...he has my eyes.

I race into my bedroom, into the closet, and I pull down a shoebox that contains some old photos.

I drop to the floor, opening up the box. I search through the family photos, some of me and Jake from high school, and then I find what I've been looking for—a picture of me from the first grade.

I hold my phone with the picture next to the photo of me at the same age.

Jesus Christ.

We look like twins.

My heart starts to pump as my cell starts to ring in my hand.

I answer, pressing the phone to my ear, my hand shaking.

"You got the picture?" she says before I get chance to speak.

"Yes."

"And?"

"And you know he looks like me. What exactly do you want from me? Money?"

"I don't want money." She sounds appalled that I even suggested it.

I guess that's when the final nail sinks into the coffin.

"I want Storm to have a chance to know his dad. That's all. Tiffany will never tell you herself. But I think Storm has a right to know who his father is."

Closing my eyes, I pinch the bridge of my nose, a sudden headache coming on.

I push to my feet, walking out of the closet, heading for my bathroom. "Does Tiffany still live in New York?" I ask.

"No, she lives in Queens."

"Give me her address."

There's a pause. I grab some aspirin out of the cabinet and swallow down two.

"Why?" she asks in a tentative voice.

"Why do you think?" I say impatiently. "You called me for a reason. That reason is so my son can know me, right?"

"Yes…" she says slowly.

"Then, give me her fucking address."

"Maybe you should call her first."

"And scare her away? No fucking way. Address now."

There's a pause, then, she says, "It's the apartment above Marie's Country Bakery on North Street in Queens."

"Got it. I'm catching a flight out tonight. Don't you dare tell her I'm coming. I don't want her running off again."

"I won't tell," she says softly.

I hang up the phone. My heart pounding, I grip the edge of the sink and stare at myself in the mirror.

I don't like what's staring back at me. I look a mess. My eyes are dark and hollow.

I have a son.

Jesus, I can't take care of myself, let alone another human being.

But I have to because I have a kid…a child that's mine.

I'm not afraid to admit that I'm fucking terrified though.

Maybe I should call Dad? Ask for his advice.

No. I want to be sure that this kid's mine before I tell my parents. Once I see him, I'll know for sure.

Who am I kidding? I already know for sure.

That kid looks exactly like me.

I could call Jake and get him to come with me.

But if I do, I know he'll talk me out of going to see Storm. He'll tell me to do it the legal way—to get my lawyer to contact the mother, get DNA tests and all that shit done first.

And I will do that.

But first, I need to see him with my own eyes.

I just need to meet him.

I need to meet my son.

Walking back into my bedroom, I click back to the picture, staring into my own blue eyes reflecting back at me, as I sit down on the edge of my bed.

I have a son. And he's beautiful.

My heart starts to race, and I notice my hands are shaking again. Worse this time.

I eye the bottle of Diazepam on my nightstand.

Just a couple to take the edge off.

Grabbing the bottle, I shake out two and then changing my mind, I increase it to four.

Walking over to my dresser, I pick up an already open half-drunk bottle of gin. Unscrewing the cap, I put the pills in my mouth and take a long drink of gin, swallowing them down.

I place the bottle back on the dresser and just stare out the window, running a hand through my hair.

I need to go to Queens, now.

Getting my phone, I check the times for a direct flight from LAX to JFK. There's a red-eye going out in a few hours.

Perfect.

Leaving my bedroom, I jog downstairs. I grab my jacket off the coat hook and my wallet and car keys off the hallway stand. Leaving my house, I lock up and head for my car parked in the driveway.

Unlocking my car, I climb in and fire her up. The headlights automatically come on in the dark. I shift the car into drive and open my security gate with the remote I keep in my car. As I pull out onto the deserted road, the gate starts to close behind me.

I press my foot on the gas, propelling me forward.

Speed—one of the things I love.

The rush of adrenaline it brings does it for me.

But if this kid is mine—*he's mine*—then I'm going to have to change things, especially the way I live.

The drugs have to go. The drinking has to stop.

I'll get clean.

Go into rehab if I have to. Do whatever is necessary.

I feel a rush of excitement, something I never thought I could feel at the thought of having a child.

Johnny Cash's "You Are My Sunshine" comes on the radio. Turning it up loud, I hum along, my fingers tapping on the wheel.

This is it. Right here, my life is going to change. I'm going to change everything for him.

Storm is my reason to be a better man.

God, Mom and Dad are going to be so excited when they find out they have a grandson.

I bring my cell to life, looking at Storm's picture again. I rest my cell on the top of the steering wheel, staring at him.

Screw not calling Jake.

I'm on my way to the airport. It's not like he can stop me anyway. I have to talk to him about this. I need to tell someone, and he's always the first person I want to tell the good stuff to.

Clicking off Storm's picture, I bring up Jake's number. I'm just about to hit dial when I see a flash of something up ahead in my peripheral vision.

A dog.

Fuck.

It all happens so quickly. Hitting my breaks, I swerve to miss the dog. My tires lock up and I clip the curb. My car spins out, hitting the barrier, and I go straight through.

Fuck no.

The car feels like it's flying.

Then, down.

Down.

And I know this is it.

I'm going to die.

I'm going to fucking die.

I'll never get to meet my son.

I never got to tell Jake or my folks about him.

I never got to meet my son.

A tear rolls down my face as I watch the ground coming fast toward me.

I shut my eyes—

ACKNOWLEDGMENTS

When I finished writing *Taming the Storm*, I knew I wasn't ready to let go of the Storm gang, especially Jake, but I wasn't sure why. I always knew there was something missing, this loose thread that needed tying up, but I wasn't quite sure what it was. Then, I realized that thread was Jonny. Jonny was pivotal to The Mighty Storm. Woven throughout all the Storm books, from the very beginning, he was there with Jake, Tom, and Denny—not in body but in mind and spirit. This story was my chance—*Jonny's* chance—to tell his story. This book might have been Jake's, but it was Jonny's, too. And Jonny's ending might not have been the HEA that you're used to from me, but it was one that I needed to tell—that Jonny and Jake needed to tell—so please don't yell at me for the tears!

While I'm here, I want to say thank you to all you Storm and Jake fans out there. Without you, none of this would have been possible. Your love for Jake and Tru has and continues to be awe-inspiring.

My amazing and patient husband—You always support me, always listen to me, never judge me. I love you.

And my children—Thank you for simply being *you*.

I have to say, the soccer conversation between Jake and JJ in the book comes from many similar conversations I've had with my soccer-mad son. And the conversation between Belle and Jake regarding Belle's "marriage" to Creed Carter, that little golden nugget came from a story my daughter told us about her "marriage" to a boy at school.

I keep my work circle small but filled with awesome people. And I'm fortunate to be able to call those awesome people friends. Trishy, Sali, Jovana, Naj, and Christine—Thank you for helping to make my books the best they can be.

Lauren, my agent, who wholeheartedly supports whichever direction I decide to take with my work—Thank you.

Bloggers—You are amazing! Thank you for everything you do.

And my readers—I have the best and most supportive readers an author could wish for. Thank you from the bottom of my heart.

ABOUT THE AUTHOR

SAMANTHA TOWLE is a *New York Times, USA Today*, and *Wall Street Journal* bestselling author. She began her first novel in 2008 while on maternity leave. She completed the manuscript five months later and hasn't stopped writing since.

She is the author of contemporary romances *The Mighty Storm, Wethering the Storm, Taming the Storm, Trouble, Revved, Revived*, and *When I Was Yours*. She has also written paranormal romances *The Bringer* and The Alexandra Jones Series. All have been penned to tunes of The Killers, Kings of Leon, Adele, The Doors, Oasis, Fleetwood Mac, Lana Del Rey, and more of her favorite musicians.

A native of Hull and a graduate of Salford University, she lives with her husband, Craig, and their son and daughter in East Yorkshire.

Made in the USA
San Bernardino, CA
22 April 2018